# CASEY'S LAST CHANCE

# Casey's Last Chance

## JOSEPH B. ATKINS

**Mojo Triangle Books™**
An Imprint Of

SARTORIS
LITERARY
GROUP

A traditional publisher
with a non-traditional approach to publishing

To my wife Suzanne
Centenio Atkins, who was
there at the novel's
conception and kept a sharp
eye on it to make sure it was
everything it could be.

"Joe Atkins's *Casey's Last Chance* is such pitch-perfect vintage noir, you can almost smell the cigarette burning in the ashtray, a woman's perfume drifting past. With a twisty plot, vibrant characters, and hardboiled grit to burn, it's everything you want in a crime novel."—**Megan Abbott, Edgar-award-winning author of *Dare Me* and *The Fever***

"Move over Greg Iles and make room for another novelist who traffics in treachery, wild rides, unreconstructed Nazis and rogue agents. In *Casey's Last Chance*, Joseph B. Atkins establishes for himself a place in the top ranks of Southern gothic storytellers, with a cast of evil characters and a few good men and women to fight them."—**Curtis Wilkie, author of *The Fall of the House of Zeus***

"Joe Atkins has crafted an original, provocative take on the 1960s South. This story has it all — mobsters, assassinations, romance, gothic landscapes, and a cast of characters you'll remember long after you've read the final sentence."—**Neil White, author of *In the Sanctuary of Outcasts***

"The sense of place in *Casey's Last Chance* is palpable. The author knows the long dark stretches of blacktop between dim lights on Mississippi secondary roads, the dangerous sections abruptly encountered in our few cities, the little towns with photographs in filling station windows of mere boys and handwritten signs that say STOP THE KILLING. You can follow Casey's route with this novel as a richly annotated road map. But take my advice. Drive a clean reliable car in daylight under the speed limit, but not too much. Speak politely if stopped. At night, I wouldn't drive Casey's route except with puncture proof tires, a bright flashlight, and a .38 caliber detective special in my glove box."—**Jere Hoar, author of *Body Parts* and *The Hit***

# CHAPTER 1

*July 1960 ...*

The night sky broke just as the Greyhound crossed the Tennessee line. Down came a blinding deluge that forced cars and trucks off to the sides of Highway 72 and under the shelter of the overpasses, but not the Memphis-bound bus that carried Casey Eubanks. He stirred through the troubled sleep that overtook him after the stop in Decatur, and stretched his arm across the newspaper in the seat next to him. He heard none of the rain that beat against the windowpane, only Clyde Point's voice in his dream.

*This is your last chance, Casey Eubanks.*

The bus braked to make the left onto Union near downtown. It was a half-hour early.

*I'm already way out on a limb talking you up to my boss like I did. He's telling the Big Guy, the Big Mahah, you're the right man for the job, but are you man enough to take the job?*

Casey woke to the lights leading up to the crest of the hill where Union crosses Front and then descends toward the Mississippi River. People huddled in doorways and under awnings. As the bus pushed through the sheets of rain, he spotted two platinum blondes at the entrance of an open garage. Their lips worked feverishly as they stabbed the air between each desperate drag of their cigarettes.

He could still hear Clyde's voice.

*You get a new life, a new identity, the cops off your back, plenty of cash in your pocket, and maybe, someday, that pool hall you used to tell me was your big dream. And you get to forget the woman who put you in this mess.*

Casey had been to Memphis before—when the sidewalks swelled with uniforms, drunk, swaggering GIs forcing the black zoot-suiters spilling off Beale Street to move to the side. He'd come with an AWOL high roller from Fort Bragg who promised to back him in a nightlong set of three-cushion, one-pocket, and straight pool at $200 a match. The high roller disappeared after he lost the second round of one-pocket, and the last thing Casey remembered was getting his head split open with a blackjack. He woke the next morning at the bottom of the levee, the Mississippi River to one side and Cotton Row to the other.

He climbed off the bus, groggy and in a bad mood.

*Do it right, and both you and me reap the rewards.*

He wanted his hotel room and his bed. Other than a few travelers and a *Commercial Appeal* hawker, the station was dead. He stopped to buy a paper. CUBAN STREET FIGHTING read one headline. His eyes moved across the page. KENNEDY OUTLINES PHILOSOPHY ON LABOR. He turned to the pages inside—EXOTIC DANCER OPENS AT THE SULTAN CLUB—then flipped from front to back, and back to front again. No news about the killing of Bux Baggett in Jonesboro, North Carolina, the woman who caused it, and the curly-headed fool who did it and who's on the lam, a hustler and pool shark with a tattoo of Rita Hayworth on each arm.

*Your last chance, Casey Eubanks.*

Casey stood at the station entrance and checked out the street. The rain had subsided. Streams of neon red and yellow reflected off the pavement. The blondes were walking eastward, their heads side-by-side under a parasol, still gesturing with their cigarettes.

In the glass window to his right, just close enough to catch the corner of his eye, he saw another fake blond, himself, an alien named James Thompson, the burial insurance salesman who'd snatched his body back in Phenix City. He studied his new self, the dyed hair, the oversized gray suit Clyde Point had given him. For a moment he felt as if he were high. High on reefer. Like the time he dropped his favorite cue stick and watched it slither across the pool table. He knew it was no snake, but he never touched that stick again. Never even looked at it.

He thought of the woman who put in the dye, the scowl in the bathroom mirror, the stubby fingers that dug through his hair like grub worms.

"Curly, you gonna look weird as hell as a blond," she'd told him. "You too dark to be a blond."

He stepped out into the steam and made his way up Union, past the golden glow of the Peabody Hotel, through the airless night, when it's a struggle even to breathe, toward what Clyde called a "little, easy-to-miss street named November 6," where he'd find his hotel.

What he found was an alley lined with trashcans and fire escapes. At the far end of it was a neon sign: *Hotel Paris*. The alley served the side door exits for every building on it except the hotel itself, four stories of stacked brick, a lean-to with nothing to lean to. It was just wide enough for three windows on each of the three floors above the lobby. As he walked toward the hotel on the oily strip of tar and asphalt, he heard the scramble of claws against the pavement.

Casey jumped the puddle in front of the entrance and opened the door. Inside was a stretch of darkness broken by a lone bulb hanging over the counter at the other end of the lobby. A clerk in a navy blue shirt and dark pinstriped vest scribbled on a notepad. A young guy, early twenties. A cigarette dangled from his lips as he stopped to hum a few notes before jotting something down. Nearby was a black vinyl couch. On the wall behind it hung a photograph of a city boulevard on an overcast day—no people, no cars, only deserted sidewalks and empty cafés.

A Swastika hung from the roof of a building. Beneath the photograph, in gold letters, was *Champs Elysées, Paris, 1941*.

An overhead fan buzzed. By the couch was an unlit stairway. *You been a small-timer all your life. Now you get to play in the big leagues.* The big leagues. A bus ticket to a cheap flophouse in a back alley.

He approached the counter.

"Name?" the clerk asked, ashes dropping from his cigarette onto his notepad. He blew them off to the side.

"James Thompson."

The clerk checked his ledger and reached below to grab a chain with a single key. He dangled it in the air. "Welcome to the Hotel Paris," he said, dropping the key into Casey's open palm. "Suite 13. Your lucky number. Bathroom's at your end of the hall."

He flipped the light and climbed the stairway to the third floor. The kid was right. His suite was next to the bathroom.

~ ~ ~

A black doorman in tails stood by the entrance of the Peabody the next morning and nodded as Casey walked in. Casey rolled his shoulders, straightened his tie, pulled his pants up level with his navel, and took in the famous lobby for the first time—its marble fountain and marble floors, colonnades and chandeliers, the stained glass ceiling, the boutiques and restaurants. A crowd had already gathered in front of the bar and at the tables around the fountain. He found a table near the piano, where a thin, white-haired man in a tux was telling a couple his next tune.

"'All Or Nothing At All,'" he said and stretched his hands across the keys.

A middle-aged waitress in a short black skirt, too old for the auburn hair that flowed down her back and across her shoulders, was at Casey's side before he could even take a seat. He ordered a CV beer and sat back and listened to the old man. He recognized the tune, something he used to hear back in the forties.

He was midway through his second CV when a man in a baggy, beige suit swaggered up to the table and took a seat like he owned it and everything around it. He looked to be sixty. His coat fell back when he sat, exposing green suspenders with golden clips.

Pulling a corona out of a pocket and plucking it in his mouth, he studied Casey before striking a match, and then he motioned to the waitress, who gave him a knowing wink. A cloud of cigar smoke drifted toward Casey, who registered the baseball-sized lump in the man's left pants pocket.

"You the important man I'm supposed to see?" Casey asked.

The piano player was finishing "I'll Never Smile Again" when the waitress returned. "Chivas Regal, double on the rocks. Like you like it, Mr. Kettle. "

He waved her away.

"You ever been to the Peabody before?" he drawled. "They got these ducks here they bring down from the roof

14

to play in that fountain over there. It's a big attraction. Tourists just love 'em."

"Sounds fascinating."

He dragged on the corona.

"But you know something? Nobody sees 'em except at the appointed time. Like the man I'm about to introduce you to."

"So who are you?"

"You hear the lady? Kettle, Tate Kettle. You got something for me? Hand it over."

Casey remembered the sealed envelope Clyde gave him. Something about Tate Kettle smelled familiar. Casey glanced at the hotel entrance and met the eyes of the doorman.

Kettle opened the envelope and read the contents with no expression, then he crunched it in his beefy hand—every other finger had a sapphire or a ruby—and shoved it into a coat pocket. Flicking the ashes of his cigar into the ashtray, he pushed his seat back and bottom-upped his Scotch.

"This fella Clyde Point, works for our friend Ike Berliner, says you perfect for the job we need done. We'll see. Must say you ain't much to look at, blondie." He tilted his head toward the elevator. "Come with me."

They rode the elevator in silence to the 12th floor, where Kettle led the way to a door with no number. A tall, lean man with a widow's peak answered his knock. "He's waiting." The man spoke with an accent.

15

They walked down a hallway and stepped into a split-level suite—a bar on the upper level, and a fireplace and shelves lined with books on the lower. Drapes blocked the sun to their left. Over the mantel was a hunting scene, jackbooted Bavarians taking aim at wild boar. In the distance stood snow-capped mountains and a castle shrouded in mist.

On the bar was a row of green and golden bottles—Armagnac, Pernod Veritas, Galliano, Anis Herbsaint. Casey had never heard of any of them, had never been in a place like this. Seen it in a movie maybe.

From a hidden passageway behind the bar came tapping. Soon a man with a cane appeared. He was in his late sixties, pale and slight, wearing a green silk robe and green bedroom slippers. Within the folds of the robe was a golden, fire-breathing dragon. He stopped and stared at Casey as he drew on a yellow, unfiltered cigarette. A scar marked his left cheek. He waved the cane toward the seats and coffee table in front of the fireplace.

"Mr. Kettle, you've brought our guest."

The English was perfect, but he and the widow's peak had the same accent.

He extended his hand to Casey but pulled it away the moment Casey touched it. "Max Duren." He smelled of expensive cologne. They sat.

*Remember you're no longer Casey Eubanks. You're James Thompson, and that's what you call yourself.*

"James Thompson."

Max Duren pulled a silver case from a pocket in his robe and offered Casey a cigarette. Casey shook his head. Duren smiled. "Black tobacco. Very strong. Perhaps too strong for your American tastes." Holding his cigarette between thumb and forefinger, he pulled a loose flake from his lip. A ribbon of smoke curled around his face.

Casey peered at Max Duren through the smoke. Seen him in a movie, too. Only thing missing was a monocle. What kind of deal had Clyde gotten him into? Not that it mattered. He was James Thompson, and this was his world.

"Something to drink? Should I have Klaus bring you some coffee? Cognac?" He snapped his fingers at the widow's peak.

"You've come to us highly recommended." Duren turned to Kettle. "What is the man's name who manages Berliner's place?"

Kettle leaned back and crossed his hands over his belly. "Point. Clyde Point."

"Yes. Strange name. How is it you know each other?"

"We go back a long way. I did him a favor once."

"One good deed deserves another, right? Well, we have an important task before us, so important I insisted on this meeting. I like to look into the eyes of those we assign important tasks."

"What do your eyes tell you?"

"Quite frankly, I'm not sure. I have to warn you. You've reached a point of no return. You understand, of course."

"I figured I reached that point when I climbed on that bus to Memphis."

"Very good and very true."

Klaus returned with a tray laden with coffee. Casey sipped from his cup and tasted mainly cognac.

"So what's the job?"

Duren exchanged glances with Kettle, took his yellow cigarette out of his mouth and stared at it. "You are to commit murder, Mr. Thompson."

The word hung in the air for a long time.

Casey nodded. He'd figured as much. He'd already done it once. He could do it again.

"You are to kill someone who has become very troublesome for us. Are you comfortable with such an assignment?"

"Who is he?"

Another exchange of glances.

"It's a woman, Mr. Thompson. A woman."

Duren twisted what remained of his cigarette into an ashtray next to the coffee. "We've been assured this would not be a problem for you. Is that correct?"

Casey shrugged. "One less bitch in the world, right?"

"Excellent. I'm going to let Mr. Kettle explain the details of your assignment. I hope, both for you and for Mr. Point, that you live up to our high expectations."

Rising from his chair, Duren took his cane and tapped it sharply on the table. "Do you love your country, Mr. Thompson?"

"What's that got to do with anything?"

"Are you a patriot?"

Casey shrugged again. "Sure, why not?"

Duren touched his finger to his lips, a flicker of curiosity in his black eyes. "You're about to do something very patriotic. Isn't that right, Mr. Kettle?"

Kettle shifted forward in his seat. "Damned right." The fire in his cigar long dead, he pulled it out of his mouth and crunched it in the ashtray. "Don't worry, Max. I'll get him up to speed."

Duren bowed to them and disappeared down the passageway behind the bar. Casey took his cup and drank it down to the grinds.

"Let me tell you something, Thompson. You've just been in the presence of a great man, a helluva lot smarter'n either you or me, you understand?"

Casey made no response. He was still processing what Duren had said.

"You probably noticed he's not from around here. The man speaks six languages, does business with people all over the world. Know where I met him? Hong Kong. Ever hear of Hong Kong, Thompson? You lucky he wanted to meet you. Shows how important this is. You do good work, he's going to remember you. Just like I will. You hear me?"

Casey figured out that smell. He'd known men like Kettle. They like you to jump every time they bark.

"You fight in the war, Thompson?"

AWOL'd twice in basic training, slugged a second louie, dishonorable discharge. Got sharpshooter in rifle practice, however. Scored a perfect 100.

Casey shook his head.

"Me neither. We weren't fighting the right people anyway. The ones we should've been fighting are still out there, wanting to take over our country. Yes, that's right. We got a war going on right now, right here at home, and we need people like Max Duren, sure as hell need 'em in the South. Duren is a man of many investments. I'm the one helped him set up shop here in Memphis. He's got a very important investment in Mississippi, just down the road, and it's being threatened, Thompson. He asked you if you love your country. I didn't quite hear your response. Do you love your goddam country, Thompson?"

"Sure, God bless America. Let's skip the speeches. Tell me about this job."

Kettle was at the edge of his chair, belly hanging over his belt, stretching the green suspenders into a half-circle.

"What we got is a real-deal communist. You know what that is, don't you?"

Casey waited.

"A communist who's telling Max Duren's workers they need to protest the way they being treated, tellin' 'em they underpaid and overworked, that they got to join a labor union. You read the newspapers, don't you? If it ain't the N-A-A-C-P, it's the goddam C-I-O trying to take over."

20

He stopped a moment, eyes bearing down on Casey. "This is more than about a little plant in the godforsaken Mississippi Delta. This is about your country."

Casey had heard enough about his country. "This country's never done a thing for me, so what do I care? I don't give a shit about the country or the South. You better start talking about what I do care about, what this deal's going to mean to me and my pocket, or I gotta elevator to catch."

Kettle stared at him a long time, then broke into a deep-bellied laugh and slapped Casey across the shoulder with his big paw. "Balls. Good. I like that. Fair enough. Forget the medals and all the rest. You sound like the kind of man I can work with." He reached into his pocket, tugged a moment at the big lump, and pulled out five one-hundred-dollar bills. He placed them one by one across Casey's leg. "Five more of these are coming to you once the job is done. If we like your work, there'll be more jobs and lots more of these."

Casey looked down at the money spread across his leg and wiped his mouth. He'd never been paid this much money for anything. Kettle watched his newly hired hit man pick up the bills, fold them, and slip them into his shirt pocket. Casey patted the pocket. Sure, he'd kill for this. Maybe for less.

Kettle laid out the plan. At noon the next day, Casey would find a 1956 white Pontiac parked in a garage off Union across the street from the Peabody. A key would be on the floorboard in the back, and a fully loaded Italian carbine in the trunk. Casey would follow Third Street onto Highway 61 and go south for 75 miles to Clarksdale. Twenty miles southwest of Clarksdale, in Percy County, he'd find a town called Spider Creek.

Kettle stopped and stared at his hire as if he were rethinking the decision. He pulled a map from a drawer in the coffee table and opened it up. "Pay close attention. You not from around here." He pointed to Spider Creek and told of a gravel lot and nearby wooded area and shed where Casey would set up.

At around six or so, people would start to gather in the lot around a flatbed thirty yards or so from the shed.

"Just a bunch of lintheads, workers at a garment factory called Bengal Britches. The factory is a couple miles away down Jefferson Davis. Most of them will be women getting off work. They'll be coming to hear the communist tell 'em how bad they got it, how a dollar an hour ain't good enough for 'em."

After going over the escape route, Kettle stood up, stepped over to the fireplace, and studied the hunters and wild boar. He spoke with his back to Casey. "Yep, it's a woman you'll kill, Thompson, but this one's the goddam whore of Babylon. You'll be doing the world a favor."

"What about cops?"

Kettle turned around with a wave of his hand. "You not gonna have no problem with cops, son. That's been taken care of. What kind of operation you think this is?"

As Kettle sat down to repeat the key details of the assignment, Casey stared off into space, into the long road

22

behind him—from Jonesboro to his first hideout in Myrtle Beach, to Phenix City, to this room in the Peabody Hotel in Memphis. Only at the end, when Kettle said, "You're a soldier, Thompson, a soldier in the New Confederacy," did the room come back into focus.

What he saw was a grin. It's a joke, the grin told him, an insider's joke, and, Casey, you've been let inside.

# CHAPTER 2

That night he found a barbecue joint near the river called Swope's. The specialty of the house arrived soaked in a red sauce that he swore was motor oil. The waiter, chief cook, and cashier had three chins and looked like he ate three meals a day at Swope's B-B-Q. He had a nasty cold and nothing to wipe his nose with but his apron.

Casey put his fork down after a couple of bites and looked through the paper while he finished off his beer. The headline **MAN IN FIERY INFERNO PLEADS FOR HELP** caught his attention. The story told of a man trapped for hours in a burning grain elevator before a helicopter was able to rescue him.

"Help! Somebody help!" the man begged friends and witnesses below. "Oh, my God, I'm going to burn to death!"

24

"Lucky for you that Whirlybird come," Casey mumbled to himself. "Your friends were lettin' you go up in smoke."

On the walk back to the hotel, he bought a pint of Evan Williams Black to get rid of the taste of Swope's barbecue. He could still smell the place. The smell clung to his clothes and to his skin.

Back in his room he threw his clothes across the chair, stretched across the bed, and listened to a corkscrew make its way through his stomach. The same interior decorator who did the lobby must have handled the rooms. Above the iron bed was another wartime photograph, in a black metal frame, this one of the Eiffel Tower, probably taken on that same cloudy day in 1941 with not a human in sight. Next to the bed was a nightstand with lamp and telephone. In the far corner stood an electric fan with blades covered in dust and a cord worn down to the wire. Down below an alley cat was in bad need of companionship.

He went over Kettle's instructions and thought about the woman in Spider Creek. Ala Gadomska was her name. Not only the whore of Babylon but a Polack Jew to boot, Kettle said. In his pocket were the five one-hundred-dollar bills. His ticket out. He dwelled on that thought as he sipped the Evan Williams. Duren had made one point perfectly clear. If he disappeared now, he would pay the price, and so would Clyde.

Casey first met Clyde over a game of eight-ball just after the war, when Clyde was a rogue deputy back in Jonesboro always looking to cut a deal. When the rogue deputy tried to squeeze his way into a liquor still business that Casey's cousin, Bux Baggett, was running, Casey warned him the sheriff himself was backing the still.

Clyde's response was to raid the place. Big mistake. He got in a roll-and-tumble fight with Bux, who was never the same after the Battle of the Bulge, and got his nose bitten nearly off. In a county run by the sheriff, Clyde's only hope was Casey, who found him a friendly doctor in Fayetteville. He came out of it with a reconstructed nose, even if his nostrils pointed out like a pig's snout. He was alive, and for that he carried a big IOU.

More than a decade later, Casey got his turn to be on the run. He was ready to collect.

Casey drank more Evan. He would see it through, do what he said he'd do, get the other five hundred—it'd be waiting for him at the Peabody front desk—and then disappear. A thousand dollars was enough to start a new life. No more barking boss man.

It was late. Sirens wailed in the distance. Somebody was in trouble, and someone was knocking on the door of Suite 13 of the Hotel Paris. The sheet stuck to his skin as he pulled himself up. He walked to the door, naked, and opened it to the songwriting desk clerk.

"Just wanted to check to make sure everything's all right," the kid said, cigarette bobbing between his lips, his eyes trailing southward. He cradled a bottle of Jamaican rum, and his breath stunk from the two-thirds of it that was missing. The shirt under his pinstriped vest was the color of Swope's barbecue sauce. His brilliantined hair curled up into a ducktail with one lock dangling down the middle of his forehead. "You found the bathroom, the towels, with no trouble?" He tried to enunciate, but rum had greased the skids.

Casey assessed the hair, the baggy tan slacks, the two-tone shoes. "Gene Vincent, right?"

The clerk was confused.

"The look. Forget it. Just need some sleep, Gene."

The kid plucked the cigarette from his mouth, dropped it to the floor, and crushed it with the pointed tip of his shoe. He still wore his high school graduation ring.

"The name is Monte, like Montezuma, the emperor of Mexico, and you, of course, are … ."

"Tired as hell and wantin' to get some sleep, Monte."

Monte leaned clumsily against the doorframe. "You're working for Duren, aren't you?"

"For who?"

Monte pulled another cigarette out of the pack in his vest pocket. He popped it in his mouth and let it hang there unlit. "The man who lives on the top floor of the Peabody."

"Where'd you hear that, Monte?"

"Memphis is a small town. " He pulled the cork on his rum and offered the bottle to Casey. "Not hard to hear things."

Casey pushed the rum away and gave him a steely grin. "Strange town, too, huh?"

Monte nodded and took a swallow. He kept the tip of the bottle at his lower lip as he spoke. "Very strange town, Mr. Thompson. I shouldn't even be talking to you like this.

Hotel rules. No fraternizing with the guests. But it gets lonely."

"So who is this Duren?"

"The King Duck, watching over his kingdom from his nest high in the sky."

He waved his hand across the invisible kingdom and stiffened his legs against the gravity that kept tugging at them.

"A duck, huh?"

"The king of the Peabody ducks," Monte said. His eyes searched the room. "May I come in, just for a bit?"

Casey's expression gave him his answer, and Monte accepted his defeat with a bow. "You're a pretty man, Mr. Thompson, in your own dark way, and I don't want anything to happen to you. Do what he asks you. Please?"

He swung toward the stairway and began his descent. Casey caught him at the third step. "Hey, Monte!"

"Yes, James?"

"Get the owner to put in some air conditioning. At least a fan that won't electrocute you."

"Tell your boss. He owns the place."

Monte pointed an imaginary gun at Casey. "Gotcha."

Casey shut the door and went back to bed. Monte, the clerk and would-be songwriter, their messenger boy. They figured Casey needed a little reminder. Maybe they were worried he would take his five hundred dollars and run. That's all right. Let them sweat, sweat like a night in the Hotel Paris.

Eventually the city grew quiet, and he drifted into more troubled sleep, back to another, long ago night a thousand miles away, in Jonesboro, North Carolina, the night he started running. It was Good Friday.

*Bux Baggett the hero, thinking you're back in the war, saving the world from Nazis. Soon as you hear her screaming, see her pink Ford parked outside that juke joint, you pull over. You're out of your head, talking crazy, taking your knife with you when you get out of the car, leaving your .32 with me and the boy.*

*"Orella Weicker's not worth it!" I tell you. "You got no stake in this. I do, and I say leave her."*

*You go in anyway, and soon after out she comes in a red dress, low cut, halfway up her thigh. Then you come. She goes down on her knees, crying, begging. For what? So I grab that .32, jump out of the car, and point it at her face.*

*"Swallow this," I tell her.*

*Only mean to scare her, teach her a lesson, so I aim high, but hero steps into the line of fire just as I pull the trigger. It's a sick, miserable mistake, Bux, but now you're on your belly bleeding your life away, Orella, looking at me with those green eyes, your blood on her naked shoulders, and me, Casey Eubanks, a dozen yards away, a crack shot, the best, your .32 pointed at the sky.*

~ ~ ~

The '56 Pontiac was where Kettle said it would be, the keys, the loaded rifle, a map, an extra box of shells. It was a two-door hardtop, white in front and on top, turquoise green along the sides and rear, New Jersey tags, a fine car, 350 V8 engine. Good on gas, too, but stripped down. No air conditioning, no radio. The tank was three-quarters full.

Steering the car onto Union, he looked up to the top of the Peabody and saw the curtained windows of Duren's penthouse. Duren was probably in his nest, still in his robe and bedroom slippers, smoking his black tobacco, savoring the thought of getting rid of his troublemaker at the factory, the communist, one of those Reds trying to take over the country, take it away from people like Max Duren and Tate Kettle.

He drove down Third Street toward Highway 61, windows down, the air blowing in hot. He drove under the Illinois Central overpass and passed a long stretch of warehouses, grocers, diners and liquor stores. A group of black men in overalls and brogans stood outside the ramshackle Hard Luck Café just off the road and watched him drive by as they shared a bottle in a brown bag.

Kettle's words echoed. *Ala Gadomska. That's a hell of a name, ain't it? What does she look like?*

*Don't worry about it. You'll know her as soon as she opens her mouth.*

Spider Creek was two hours away. He needed to get there early enough to establish the layout of the place, fix his escape route, and set up, but he had plenty of time. He drove through the south side of Memphis like a Sunday driver, in no hurry passing from city to country, from red brick warehouses to cinderblock car shops and makeshift stands selling hot dogs and boiled peanuts. At a stoplight he watched a team of grease monkeys swarm over a sky blue, brand new Corvette convertible, rubbing her fiberglass curves like they were caressing a woman. They had a portable radio close by. "Stay!" Maurice Williams and the Zodiacs. He reached for the radio then remembered the Pontiac didn't have one.

To the side of the Corvette stood a couple, blond and beautiful, ascot and scarf, shades and cigarettes, thin-lipped and waiting. An "Ole Miss" sticker was on the car's rear bumper. "Seven miles a gallon," Casey muttered from the driver's seat of his '56 Pontiac. "Seven."

The smiling face of Mary Ann Mobly met him at the state line. "Welcome to Mississippi!" she told him from a couple dozen feet in the air. Behind her lay thousands of acres of pancake-flat fields of still-green cotton that stretched into the horizon, vast and unbroken except for a lonely shotgun shack here and there or a lightning-struck willow oak, wilted, jagged and dead, both shack and tree leaning against the sky like old drunks. Every few miles was a juke joint, nothing more than another tin-plated lean-to with a name like "Blue Moon Club" or "Blue Light Café" painted across its slanted roof.

Mississippi reminded Casey a little of eastern North Carolina with its tarpaper shacks, dusty turn rows, and lonely graveyards. But this was worse. This was the end of the world, a chunk of hell flat-ironed onto the earth. Even the air smelled of sulfur.

"Welcome to Hell," Casey said, rolling up his window against the hot wind.

Between Tunica and Lula the highway was dead except for the occasional tractor, tractor-trailer, or pick-up truck with a grizzled-faced farmer hovering over the

31

steering wheel.    Another giant billboard loomed ahead from out of a cotton field: "Save Our Republic! Impeach Earl Warren!" Beyond the sign were a row of shotgun houses and a church. A lone post held up the sagging front porch roof of the Nazarene Pentecostal Temple of the Holy Ghost. The other post lay on the ground off to the side.

In the silence inside the Pontiac, the passing landscape was like a broken mirror. He thought of the old woman who put him in prison for a year. She testified he stole her jewelry when he broke into her house. Damned lie. He couldn't find any. She made that claim to get the insurance money. Of course, he bragged to Orella he had the diamonds stashed away. He liked putting on a show for her. When Frank Wetzel took out those two highway patrolmen, she waited up for Casey all night thinking he might be mixed up in it. He let her think it.

He'd have a story for her now, a big show for real, but she wasn't waiting for him, and he wasn't coming home. He was never going home.

He passed through the eastern edge of Clarksdale, stopping at a crossroads. The front porch of a country store off to the right offered shade from the sun to a row of cotton-haired black men waving away flies and heat with their handkerchiefs. One of them wore a cap with the Prince Albert tobacco logo. Another had a Panama hat that matched his suit. He was talking excitedly and at one point raised his hand with a great flourish before poking a long, bent index finger in the open Bible he was holding.  A white man in overalls, his cap pushed back, leaned against a column and shook his head with an amused look. He glanced toward the road just in time to catch Casey taking off and waved with a big grin.

A dozen miles south of Clarksdale Casey began looking for the turnoff to Spider Creek. He should have paid closer attention to Kettle's directions. As he slowed to check the map, a sky blue 1960 Corvette filled his rearview mirror.

Prom Queen laughed and tossed her hair back as College Boy punched the horn with the heel of his palm. The fuel-injected engine revved up, and within seconds the Corvette was side-by-side with the '56 Pontiac. Prom Queen blew Casey a kiss as both he and College Boy watched a northbound semi tractor trailer appear in the distance.

Casey held steady at sixty, figuring the Corvette would pass. College Boy was having fun, however. He pulled far enough ahead to give Casey another look at his "Ole Miss" sticker, and then he fell back again. They stayed even as the 18-wheeler grew larger. College Boy gunned the Corvette, and Casey gunned the Pontiac. The semi's horn was bellowing when the Corvette shot ahead and cut into the southbound lane. He cut so sharply that he forced Casey off the highway onto a gravel lot.

The Pontiac was within yards of a tamale stand before Casey brought it to a stop.

"Put you in my crosshairs, College Boy," he yelled at the disappearing Corvette. "Your girlfriend, too."

"New Jersey, huh."

He turned and saw a bald-headed, olive-skinned man walking toward him from the stand. He wore an open-collared, Caribbean-style shirt, and his week-old whiskers were flecked with gray. "My niece used to live up there. Long way from home."

The man spoke in a back-of-the-throat singsong. "That was a close call you just had. Youngsters think they own the road."

Casey cut the motor. "I wanted to run 'em into that semi," he told the empty highway. "I wish I hadda."

"You probably wondering what's a tamale stand doing in the middle of the Delta. The Mexicanos brought the tamales here way back. They worked this land long time ago, before I was even born. Tamales been here ever since. Let me get you one, on the house."

Casey checked the map, the turnoff that led to Highway 1 and Spider Creek.

"I got a Chinese lady gets up at five in the morning to make and wrap these tamales for me. My sister used to do it, but she's dead. Had cancer in her private parts. She and me planted the cornfield where we get the shucks to wrap 'em with. Big stand of corn back of our house. You from New Jersey, huh? How about that tamale?"

Listening to the man was enough to make you beg for mercy. The words came in the cadence you might hear in a mental institution. Little brown bubbles of snuff collected at the corners of his mouth. An eight-inch tin of Tube Rose stood on one end of the counter at the stand.

"Not hungry, old man. Need directions." Casey held up the map and pointed to Spider Creek. "Where's the turnoff that'll get me there?"

"You here 'cause of the union?"

"What union?"

"Down at Bengal Britches. That's all the folks talking about. My niece Roseanne works there. They got a big rally today."

The man's face was inches from Casey's, and his breath stunk of Tube Rose.

"Roseanne says they treat the ladies there worse than the colored, always threatening if they complain, tellin' 'em plenty others out there to take their place. 'Course ain't many jobs around here. Machines do most of the work. People movin' out, white as well as black. Mr. Kettle and me going to be the last white men in the Delta things keep going like they are."

He started giggling, spraying tiny beads of saliva and snuff.

"Back off, goddamit! You're spitting all over me."

Baldy kept giggling but wiped his mouth and backed away. "I'm sorry, mister." He stuck out his hand. Casey waved it away. "My name is Demetrie, Demetrie Giannini, but most people just call me D.G. Just an old dago. That's me."

Casey weighed whether to risk more water torture. "So who's this Kettle?"

"You never heard of Mr. Kettle? Oh, well, of course. You not from here." He stepped back farther, stretched out his arms and swung them around in all directions. "See all this? He owns it, every bit of it. He owns everything you can see from any direction."

Casey nodded up toward the sky. "He own that? He own the sky?"

"That gin, the cotton, Spider Creek. Sky, too, for all I know."

"He own the plant?"

The question confused the man at first. He had to sort through it. "Naw, he don't own the plant. That's the Germans. They got their fingers in lots of pies around the Delta, from the Memphis port to Vicksburg, from cut-and-sew to the timber business. They hand in glove with Kettle, though."

"How come you know so much?

Demetrie touched his bald head with his forefinger. "D.G. may be a crazy dago, but he's crazy smart."

"So what's the deal with the union?"

"Roseanne says they work the stretch-out all the time. You don't make it, they cut your pay or lay you off. Don't even let 'em go the bathroom when they got to. Their time of the month come, don't mean nothing. Going to vote tomorrow on bringing the union in. They been trying to get that vote for a couple years, and now they finally got it. Roseanne's voting yes. I told her she better be careful. Mr. Kettle and the Germans ain't puttin' up with no union around here. The paper says union nothing but Reds and Communists. Paper says you let the Reds in and next day they'll unionize the cotton choppers. They tried that once, but Tate Kettle's white sheet boys put an end to it."

Casey pointed to the map. "Where's that turnoff?"

Demetrie laughed. "New Jersey, huh. You don't sound New Jersey. You close, Mister. Exactly half-dozen miles straight down the highway and you'll see it."

The Pontiac fired.

"Roseanne lived in New Jersey once. Fell in love with a private first class and followed him all the way to Fort Dix. He dumped her as soon as he got discharged, and she came back home with a belly riper'n a frost-covered pumpkin. Roseanne was always book smart but dumb in love. Was going to go to business college, be a court stenographer. Just a linthead now."

"Maybe that's all she was meant to be, old timer, a linthead."

Casey shifted into gear and pulled away.

Demetrie waved goodbye.

The turnoff was where Demetrie said, and it led to a sign that was nailed to a creosote pole at Jefferson Davis Road. Scrawled across it were the words *Spider Crek*. The sign painter wasn't much of a speller.

He took Jefferson Davis into town, continuing along its east side, a block off Main Street and just west of a bayou that meandered through weeds as tall as a man. The town was dead. The first sign of life were two black pickups parked to the side of a club called Jake's at the intersection with Forrest Road. The rally was to take place in the open lot behind Jake's.

The club was a converted warehouse with no windows on its north side, just a narrow door to the right, where the two trucks were parked. He made a left onto Forrest, driving slowly past Jake's and the dirt road leading into the patch of woods where Kettle told him to set up. He continued until he came to Highway 61. He pulled over to check the map against Kettle's instructions for the getaway, which were to go south on 61 and then east to Highway 49, where he could double back to Memphis.

After a U-turn he was back on Forrest and soon onto the hidden road that ran parallel to the lot behind Jake's. He found the storage shed Kettle had described, made a circle, and parked with the nose of the car facing north. Beyond the trees lay the earthen, baseball field-sized lot, empty except for a 30-foot flatbed less than fifty yards away.

He took off his coat, leaving the .32 in the inside pocket, laid it over the backrest on the driver's side, got out, and grabbed the rifle out of the trunk. He noticed for the first time the age of the gun. The barrel was worn and scratched, and the wood stock was so loose he'd have to hold it tight when he fingered the trigger. Weeds and bush were thick around the metal shed. He had to push his way through them, holding his rifle high and stepping carefully in case of snakes. He had a while to wait so he took his time finding a spot where he could crouch down and have a clear view. He didn't think anyone could see him from the flatbed.

A line of trees and thick undergrowth stretched the full length of the lot's eastern and southern borders. The ground was still wet from the recent rains. His rifle propped over his knees, he reached down and grabbed a chunk of the thick, loamy earth, and it clung to his hand. Full of stems and leaves and the wings and legs of decaying insects, it stunk of birth and death and farm chemicals, dirt owned by Tate Kettle and maybe the Germans, too. *Everything you can see from any direction.*

The crazy dago had a voice like the radio preacher J. Vernon McGee. Orella was always listening to him and his Church of the Open Door. One of his sermons came to mind. We all walk through the valley of death every day of our lives, the preacher preached.

Casey spit hard onto the ground. *That's where you are, Ala Gadomska. The valley of death.* He said it to himself, the words rumbling inside his mouth.

The setting sun hid itself behind thickening clouds. He checked his watch. It was past six. A long shift. He searched the lot for posters or signs announcing the rally and found none. Maybe the union didn't want to stir up the Klan or whoever else might come to spoil things.

As he stood to stretch, the first pickup appeared at the south corner of Jake's and rolled across the lot. Others followed, and he crouched down into the weeds. Day shift had ended. Ten-year-old Studebakers and Fords pulled in, even an Edsel, full of rust spots around the fender. Motors rattled with bad gas. Glasspack mufflers popped. Webb Pierce's high-lonesome cried "Wonderin', Wonderin'" from a radio somewhere.

Like a silent army, the Bengal Britches workers climbed out of their jalopies and walked toward the flatbed. Bluejeans and capris pants, cotton blouses and untucked flannel shirts—all familiar to Casey. Boyfriends, brothers, and fathers stayed back behind their steering wheels. The women walked on tired legs stiff from standing on concrete floors for ten hours. The arms of the older ones hung at their sides as if too heavy to lift. The younger ones talked between drags on their cigarettes and sips from their bottles of pop. They talked to the expressionless faces beside them.

An orange-haired woman with pale skin and a rosebud mouth caught Casey's attention. She looked like Orella after she ruined her red hair with platinum. The handful of men among the women wore khakis and overalls, stick-like men with lumps of chewing tobacco in their mouths. They were the machine shop boys, the loading dock crew.

A sprinkling of blacks, most of them women, stood at the fringes. They swept the floors, dumped the garbage, cleaned out the bathrooms.

Casey studied the faces. Even from his spot he could see the pasty paleness, the cheek-to-jowl worry lines, the flat breasts and flat hair, or the sagging flesh that came with too many kids and too much hoecake. He knew these people, knew their look. They were everywhere back in the Carolinas, every small town and backwater. They came out of the hollows to work in the mills, walked off dirt farms to punch a card and pull a paycheck.

His mother had been one of them. Julep and her curly-headed, dark-skinned boy had moved into the mill village in Jonesboro after his grandfather kicked them off the farm. Casey watched the look grow on her over the years, settling into her eyes and her forehead, working its way down the line of her cheeks into the chin and neck.

Orella was one, too. She'd ask Casey to massage her feet at night while she rubbed what she called the "rigor mortis" out of her hands and fingers. The heat off her calluses made his hands sweat. That's what she got for

40

working at McDavie's Mills—calluses plus a dollar an hour.

Still, this wasn't Carolina. This was flat country, the flattest Casey had ever seen. No dirt farms here, just plantations with poor blacks and rich whites like Tate Kettle who no longer needed plenty of hands to pick his cotton. These people must have come from miles around, desperate for a job, from every dusty crossroads town where their men worked the little stores, the car shops, or not at all, people you'd never know even existed if it weren't for this plant.

And here they'd come to hear a Polack named Gadomska.

As if on cue, a red-and-white '55 Ford Crown Victoria appeared at the corner of Jake's. A man was driving, and a woman sat in the passenger seat. It turned toward the eastern border, away from the crowd, and crept along the same line of trees that hid the shed and Casey. He crouched lower as the car approached. It slowed when it came even with the flatbed, and the driver pulled alongside the attached trailer hitch.

Every eye watched the Ford's front doors open. Out of the driver's side climbed a square-faced man, short and stocky, wearing a loose-collared, short-sleeved, checkered shirt and baggy tan pants. The door on the passenger's side opened next and out stepped a tall strawberry blonde, in her late twenties, with a pretty face and shoulders slightly too broad for her small waist and slim figure. She wore jeans and a loose-fitting blue work shirt that tightened around the rise of her breasts. Her hair was wavy and cut short. She grabbed a stack of leaflets off the front seat and immediately began handing them out as she followed the man to the flatbed.

A heavyset woman in overalls stretched out her arms to take them when the blonde reached the makeshift stage. Her driver reached over to help her up, but she waved him away and swung her long legs onto the wooden platform. With people still arriving, the crowd had swelled to a hundred or more.

Casey shifted into position. Using the side of the shed as a brace, he lifted the rifle to his shoulder and stared down the long steel barrel, moving it slightly to the left, then to the right, to get her in the sight. Her friend kept stepping in and out of the way as he paced the platform. He was her bodyguard as well as her driver, muscled, bandy-legged, a belly as round and hard as a watermelon. He turned in Casey's direction a couple of times, pokerfaced, a Chinaman look about him, and then he scanned the crowd and the stragglers still coming in.

Casey sensed something when the bodyguard looked off in the distance at Jake's and flinched his shoulders. The place looked like a shutdown fortress. The doors on each end and the old loading gate in the middle were closed.

A face flashed in one of the windows but then quickly disappeared. Something besides posters was missing from the scene. Cops. Not a single blue light anywhere. Kettle had promised no problem with cops. The bodyguard was trying to figure it out. Labor rallies were like Klan rallies, guaranteed to bring out the uniforms, shades, and swagger sticks.

The bodyguard leaned over and whispered something in the woman's ear. She nodded before stepping closer to the edge of the flatbed. Looking out across the crowd, she waved at one or two of the women in the back and motioned for them to move in closer. She had no microphone.

"Another hard day today, right?" she called out, the voice strong and clear in the breeze coming across the lot.

A few exchanged looks.

"What time didya start? Six? Some earlier? Now you're just getting here. Twelve-hour day. They got a big order in, we know that. You'll be working ten, twelve-hour days next couple of weeks. Then, when the order's done, maybe not at all for a while. What your sweat and sore backs get you? Sixty cents an hour? Maybe less, huh? They don't pay you for that twenty-minute lunch break, do they? Not even for that ten-minute bathroom break.

"So what you earned today was a whoopin' six dollars and ninety cents, not a penny for the four hours overtime they should be payin' you. Bengal Britches doesn't pay overtime. They told you that when they hired you, didn't they? You agreed to it because you needed the job. Well, they're supposed to pay you. What can you do with six dollars and ninety cents? That gonna feed your family, pay the rent, put gas in the car? If your husband's out of work, it better. You got no choice, right? Well, that's what they tell you."

People edged closer to the flatbed. The woman's words hung in the air, carried by the breeze, a lot of Chicago and a hint of Poland in them—dollar was dahluh,

43

and hour was ahwuh—but somehow not Yankee hard or Yankee strange. She talked like she just came off the line herself. The bodyguard stood to her left, restless, his arms crossed, legs spread but flexing forth and back.

"And what was your day like? Still got you on the stretch-out, don't they? What's it gone to now?" She pointed to a woman three or four rows back. The woman acknowledged her with a wan smile. "Helen, I see you out there. I knew you'd come. I knew you wouldn't disappoint me. What's been production in your section? Forty dozen pairs of double-seams a day, right? Forty-five, maybe. Hard enough to make that. The stretch-out ups that to what? Sixty, seventy? You have to go so fast your hands are a blur. Hurts you at night just to lift a fork at the dinner table, doesn't it? Or when you pull back the covers on your bed. Am I right?"

Helen nodded.

"It'll be eighty we lose this vote!" the woman in overalls shouted. "Eighty, and there ain't a human can do it!"

She put her arm around another woman with a drawn face and a bulging belly under her dark brown sweater.

"Janie here has fainted twice this week tryin' to keep up. Seven months pregnant, but that don't make a difference to them. They told her to quit if she can't handle the work."

The crowd stirred. Other arms slid around Janie's shoulders, and she looked embarrassed.

Gadomska wiped her forehead and mouth before speaking again. "What'd they tell you, Janie? There's

44

plenty more where you come from, right? You're just a linthead, right? That's all you are. Something like that. That's what they told me when I was doing what you are doing. Oh, yeah. I worked the mills just like you, up North, in Chicago. Just like my mama and my daddy did back in Poland. Like many of you, they moved off the farm into the mills, broke their backs working for little or nothing. Then the Nazis came. My parents saw what was ahead, and that's why they arranged to send me to America, to be with cousins. They couldn't save themselves, but they saved me, and they died doing it. I came to America like a lot of Polish people, heart-broken, scared to death, but with lots of little girl dreams. I wasn't even out of school before I was behind a sewing machine, stitching pants while fending off a boss who thought it was his right to get into mine."

People shook their heads, jostled one another, cursed bosses current and past.

Casey waited. The bodyguard finally settled into his spot to Gadomska's left. With a clear shot in front of him, Casey steadied his gun and slipped his forefinger over the trigger.

"Scared to death, that's right. You all know what that is, don't you? Scared of losing your job, scared of your boss, scared to stand up for yourself. I'll tell you, and I'm not bragging, I'm not scared any more. Not of a damned thing. My good friend Wlodek here worries about me. I say, 'Wlodek, how can I tell them not to be afraid if I'm afraid?' I look at your faces and I think of the other mill workers I've known in my life. It doesn't matter whether it's Mississippi, the Carolinas, Chicago, or Lodz, the city of my mother and my father in Poland. We're just people, all of us. It took me a long time to realize that, to realize I'm a human being, that I got rights God gave me as a human being. The boss never talked about that. He talked about what his rights were. That's for sure. What makes him better than me? He looks down, and I'm supposed to look up? I couldn't see what was right in front of my eyes. People had to help me. It's so hard to do it alone, to stand alone. You have no power, no say so when you stand alone. I couldn't stand up to the forces controlling my life when it was just me. And neither can you. There's no way. The only way to stand up to them is with other people just like you. That's why I joined the union. That's why you need a union, and why you need to vote `Yes!' tomorrow. Change your life tomorrow! Never be afraid again! Stand up together! Vote `Yes'!"

The women burst into applause and raised their fists in the air.

Casey stared down the sight of the rifle at the back of Ala Gadomska's head. *Just a linthead.* He gripped the gun and settled on a spot at the base of her skull. Occasionally she moved from side to side as she spoke, but then she stopped and stood still as if purposely, as if to give him the perfect shot. His finger rubbed against the trigger. The moment had come. He shifted, readjusted his shoulders, eyed his target. *The whore of Babylon. Doing the world a favor.* She began to pace. He raised his eyes and in the faces in the crowd again saw Julep, that dim-witted, purposeless grin that had been hers all his life, like that itch between her legs, saw Orella, the peach-bottomed preacher's wife who turned linthead after the reverend took off.

Ala Gadomska came to a standstill.

*Shoot me, Casey Eubanks.*

He shifted again, braced, took aim. Beads of sweat lined his forehead. He was short of breath. It was time to pull the trigger, but his finger wouldn't move. Ala Gadomska's voice filled the space around him until he hated the sound of her voice. He wanted her to shut up, and he had the means to make her, but he couldn't pull the trigger.

Lowering the gun a moment, he tried to take a deep breath, wiped his forehead. He raised it again. His eyes burned. She was clear in his sight, standing still, her bodyguard to her side, but Casey's finger would not pull the trigger. The barrel was pointed directly at his target, but he couldn't do what he'd come to do. He had the perfect shot, but he could not kill Ala Gadomska.

He stepped back through the thick brush and wisteria. The mud sucked at his feet. The cold steel of the rifle and the unspent shell in its barrel mocked him. He looked across the lot at Ala Gadomska. She still hadn't moved. He stood up and clicked the safety on the gun. The barrel hung down by his side like a limp dick. Casey Eubanks had the best eye of any man he knew. He'd learned how to hunt from the best, his cousin Watt Critchfield. Casey Eubanks could kill a squirrel poking its head around the backside of a tree at sixty yards. He could pocket a three-cushion shot because he knew exactly where to hit the ball and what it would do when he did. Yet he'd killed Bux Baggett with a fluke shot meant to singe the hair of the woman who betrayed him. And with a clear target in the sights on a flatbed just forty yards away, he'd frozen.

The smell of cheap after-shave drifted past him.

"Thought you came down here to do a job."

He swung around and found himself staring into the twin barrels of a sawed-off shotgun.

# CHAPTER 3

He was a stump of a man, a cop in his dark blues, leaning against the Pontiac with a crooked grin on his round baby face. He reached for the pack of Mail Pouch tobacco in his shirt, holding the shotgun steady. He spat out his used wad.

"Not up to it, huh?" The voice was high-pitched like a girl's.

Casey scanned the dirt road, the tree line, searching for a patrol car. Must be hidden deeper in the woods behind trees and brush. The cop must have gotten there before Casey did. Must have known Casey was coming and where he would set up. Must have been waiting for him.

"Don't have the belly to shoot the bitch on the flatbed?"

The cop chuckled, dug into the Mail Pouch, enjoying the moment. He stuck his new wad inside his mouth and pushed it to the side.

"Don't worry about it. Our little secret. Here's what I'm going to do for you. I'm going to go ahead and kill you. Got to do it just to save her life, right? That'll be our story. The world will never know you were chicken shit."

As he lifted the shotgun to eye level, something moved in the trees and bushes to Casey's left. The cop turned, giving Casey the moment he was waiting for, the three seconds needed to take the safety off his rifle, snap it forward, and blast that grin into eternity.

He had no trouble pulling the trigger this time, and he found his mark. Baby Face blanched with shock as his knees buckled and he slumped to the ground. His weapon fell to the side. Blood sprouted from the hole in his chest.

Casey stepped closer. Dying eyes gazed up at him, the image of a last unanswered question fixed on them like an undeveloped negative. *What happened?* Casey reached down, picked up the pack of Mail Pouch, and tossed it into the brush.

"Bad for your health, bud," he said to the man who wanted to kill him. He tried to laugh, but he had no laughter in him. A dead man lay at his feet. The second man dead because of Casey Eubanks. Voices in the distance reminded him of the flatbed. He swung around and saw people crouching, some still scurrying for cover. Several pointed in Casey's direction. No sign of the woman and her bodyguard.

He popped the empty shell out of the rifle and shoved another into the barrel from the clip. Grabbing the cop's arm, he stumbled as he pulled the dead weight away from the Pontiac. The crunch of brush a few yards behind him made him release his grip and turn just as the bodyguard lunged midair at him.

Casey moved fast, lifting the rifle with both hands and firing into the man's left shoulder. The bodyguard fell to the ground, the arm hanging useless at his side, the other groping at Casey's feet. Before Casey could load another shell, Ala Gadomska was on him like a banshee out of hell, scratching and kicking.

Caught off guard and shaken by her strength, he struggled to pull her away but her nails were already deep enough in him to draw blood. He managed to step back to the car door and toss the rifle on the floorboard. As he reached for the steering wheel, a set of perfect Polish teeth stopped him cold with a vicious crunch, incisor to molar, into his shoulder.

"Damn you!" he shouted as she bit down harder. Flailing about in pain, he grabbed a chunk of strawberry blond hair and violently pulled back, slightly loosening his grip when he glimpsed her green eyes and the look of rage in them.

Unbelievably she immediately threw a jab that he ducked just in time, and he back-fisted her on the ball of her cheek. Something flashed in his brain as she sank into unconsciousness, and he grabbed her with both hands and threw her into the front seat of the car. Hearing others now running toward the scene, he jumped in, pushing her to the passenger's side, and turned the ignition so hard it rattled in defiance.

But the Pontiac quickly came to life, and he shoved it into first gear and spun off, spraying baseball-sized chunks of black earth at the first men to emerge from the bushes. The Pontiac sped down the dirt road and with tires screeching took the 90-degree turn onto Forrest.

Even with one foot on the brake, Casey never stopped pumping the accelerator, making the engine roar at the next hard right onto 61. He was a mile south of that turn before the first clear thought came, the need to stay off the main roads. Kettle's instructions were meaningless now, and his brain raced as fast as the Pontiac searching for an eastbound exit.

~ ~ ~

Night had fallen, and the string of road spiraled into it, bending left then right, through clouds of flying bugs, between bayous and shadows of trees, as if it might disappear at any moment and leave him lost in a sea of blackness. He tried to focus but the ball peen hammer pounding inside his head made it hard. His temples throbbed. His eyes hurt. The '56 Pontiac strained under the constant pumping and breaking, but he couldn't risk slowing down. He was lost—again. In the engine's whine he could hear the keening of a woman, her mouth a gaping wound, on her knees in front of a faraway juke joint, and he cursed himself.

*You got it all wrong, Casey.* That's what Orella's lips had said against the bonfire lighting up the sky behind her that other, long ago night, exposing her nakedness under that sheer red dress. *All wrong*, she'd repeated just before he turned and jumped into her pink Ford with the keys still in the ignition. *You got it all wrong.*

Dressed like a streetwalker, mascara smeared across her face, on her knees, and she wanted him to believe he had it all wrong. Some regulars at the pool hall had told him long before that night they heard she went there. He nearly took the head off one of them for saying it. All the man did was tell the truth.

He leaned into the steering wheel as he negotiated the narrow bridges over scrub-and-vine-canopied creeks. He struggled to keep his mind straight, to concentrate, so he could decide his next step.

Night descends like a blanket in the Delta, covering nearly everything. Delta roads are unlit. Plantation homes are behind the horizon. Only the occasional gas station or kerosene lamp in the window of some woebegone shack rends the shroud that is a Delta night. When none is in view, when it's July and the sky is moonless and starless like this night, the Delta is a catacomb with no exit, as narrow as the beam from a headlight yet also endless, a sea of blackness.

He had five hundred bucks in his pocket, a half tank of gas, a loaded .32 and a rifle, and the Pontiac was the only car in sight in either direction. He also had an inflamed wound on his shoulder that stung like hell, and

53

the cause of it was coming to, groaning softly, her face twisting against the pain from the bruise on her cheek. He had popped her hard enough to put the lights out in a two-hundred-pound man. She could take a punch.

In the yellow glow from the dashboard she looked unreal, a trick his mind was playing on him. She was real all right. Tough as she was, she had soft, cream-colored skin. The scuffle had loosened a couple of the buttons on her work shirt, exposing the curve of her breast, a glimmer of pink around the nipple. A silver locket shaped like a rose hung from her neck.

He pulled the rifle up from the floorboard to his lap. Sweat dripped from his forehead, down his eyebrows, around the balls of his cheeks, into the corners of his mouth. He tried to roll the window down, but it jammed a few inches from the top. Another casualty of his fight with Ala Gadomska. He rested his head against the crack and let the hot air blow across his face.

The blacker the Delta got the better Casey saw the double cross. *Thought you came down here to do a job.* He'd played the sucker one more time. Hidden patrol car. Sawed-off double-barreled shotgun. Baby Face had been sent on a mission. Casey walked into it like a buck strolling in front of a deer stand, only the hunter in this stand knew the buck was coming long before he saw him. The cop knew why Casey was there. He knew because he was working for the same man. The wind whistled through the crack in the car window, a stinking chemist's brew.

Bugs swarmed in a frenzy across the beams of the Pontiac's headlights. Deep inside him, a screwworm gnawed at the lining of his belly. He had to hand it to Duren and Tate Kettle. They set up the perfect fix. Casey kills Ala Gadomska, The cop kills Casey, Duren gets rid of his union organizer, and his bought-and-paid-for cops close the case with a bonus for Baby Face. What was it Kettle said? *You ain't going to have no problem with cops, son. That's been taken care of.*

He followed the thread back further, all the way to his old friend Clyde Point, the man who owed him a favor. *The Big Mahah's got a job needs to be done. Sure, he's got people who could do it, but I think you'd do it better.* The perfect double cross. Clyde pays off his IOU and makes good with the boss by sending Duren the perfect patsy, a man on the run with no friends and so desperate he'll do anything, a crack shot to boot. Casey's ticket to the Big Time becomes Clyde's passport to the good graces of the Big Mahah.

A bitter smile crossed Casey's face, a sucker's smile. He looked in the rearview mirror, at the sucker staring back at him. Then he slammed the palm of his hand into it, cracking it. Bust that damned face, the Big Shot who liked to make Orella think he was Machine Gun Kelly and John Dillinger rolled into one, liked to show her the switchblade he'd won off some loser, his bruised knuckles, nothing more than a night's work handling drunk eyeballers at a third-rate pool joint.

"You're a damned fool and that's all you are!" he told the sucker in the rearview mirror.

"Where are you taking me?"

He snapped his head around to a pair of green eyes wired to his. She looked tough and sounded tough, but she was in her corner, as far from him as she could get, betrayed by a tremor that danced along her cheekbone, the squeezed-out way she said *taking*.

"Who are you? Why are you doing this?" she demanded. Her fingers traced the bruise on her face.

The strip of road coursed through the night. If only he could peel it back, peel back everything that had happened, get back to the other side of the nightmare that began a thousand miles away in what seemed another lifetime.

"Are you going to **kill** me?" she cried out, pushing herself up from her corner with both fists as if ready to spring on him.

So she wondered if he would still kill her?

She didn't know he couldn't pull the trigger earlier when he had her in the sights of that rifle? She ought to thank him she's still breathing, that she's not dead with a shell in her Polack brain. What was he supposed to tell her? That twenty-four hours ago he didn't know who the hell she was? The ball peen hammer struck again. One eye squeezed shut. The other stayed open—on the road in front of him, on the gloom behind him in the rearview mirror. They could be waiting at the next intersection, or coming around that last curve.

He lifted the .32 to a direct line with her face. "That depends on you."

He looked at her. Men become fools for such a woman—oval face, swollen lips, pug nose, skin soft and bathed in yellow light, the scent of talcum and sweat. Green eyes. She turned away, looked down at the blood on her shirt. She began to button it distractedly, deep in thought now.

The Pontiac penetrated still deeper into the Delta wilderness. Miles passed with no marker of any kind, intersections with no signs. At one point, the road divided into an anonymous Y. Casey veered left, pushing the Pontiac harder.

"I know what happened back there. I know what you did, and I know what you didn't do."

A deer darted across the beam of light just yards in front of him. He braced for others. None came.

"The police chief wanted to know if we needed protection. We had to laugh. We needed protection all right—from the police, not by the police." She touched the bruise again as she spoke. "They're controlled by the same people. You know that, don't you? The people who run the company own the town. When the chief called and made his offer, Wlodek warned me something might happen. What could we do? The workers depend on us. They vote tomorrow." She stopped a moment. "You hurt Wlodek, maybe badly ...."

The bodyguard.

"I nicked him in the shoulder, probably went straight through him. He's all right."

She shook her head. "You have to let me go. I need to know about Wlodek, and I need be there for the vote."

She edged closer. "You have to let me go!"

Casey put the pistol within a couple inches of her face. In a sudden rage, she reached up and shoved the weapon away, catching Casey off guard and forcing him to pull to the right. The Pontiac swerved and barely missed an embankment that separated the road from a cotton field. Righting the car, he stuck the .32 flush against her mouth.

"Listen, goddamit, I'll kill you all right!"

"Then why didn't you?" she shot back, pushing the gun away once more. "That's what you were hired to do. That's why you were there, hiding in the bushes. You were waiting to shoot me. When I saw you standing over that cop's body, my first thought was that he had tried to stop it. That's why I attacked you. That's why Wlodek attacked you."

The heat of her stare made his teeth grind. He was sick of her questions, her demands, her voice, her green eyes.

"But that was wrong. The cop wasn't protecting me. He was making sure you did your job, and when you did, he would do his."

She had figured it out, and the patsy had nothing to say.

She moved closer to the windshield to get a better look at his face. His shoulder throbbed where she bit him.

"It had to be that way. He knew exactly where to find you. I know I'm right because I'm still alive. You couldn't do it, could you? You couldn't kill me."

He watched the road. He drove.

"You killed the cop because that's what he was going to do to you."

Her eyes shifted to the cracked rearview mirror. "They set you up, didn't they? That's why just now you called yourself a fool. I'm right. I know I am."

The space between them shrank.

"Why did you shove me in the car?" Her voice was softer now. "Why did you take me with you?"

Silence. A quarter mile of it.

"Why? Why didn' you …?"

"Just shut the hell up," he said wearily.

She shook her head. "You don't know, do you? You don't know yourself."

They sat there, inches apart on their tiny island in the Delta sea. She leaned back, closed her eyes, and sighed. Casey lowered the pistol and slipped it under his belt.

A sign appeared at an intersection up ahead. An arrow pointed north. Three miles to Brazil. Just beyond it was another sign, a bridge over the Tallahatchie River. The Pontiac slowed. Ala Gadomska gripped the door handle as the car pulled onto a dirt clearing to the right just before the bridge.

When the Pontiac came to a halt, the headlights lit up a path sandwiched between a steel ramp to the left and a line of honeysuckle bush to the right. The path led downhill past the trestlework to the river below.

Casey shoved the gear stick into neutral and kicked the emergency brake. He left the motor running with the lights on.

"Get out of the car."

His hands remained on the steering wheel. She moved her lips to say something, but held back. The door opened, and she swung to the right and stepped onto the ground.

"I know ... someone who can help you," she said, facing the night.

"Shut the hell up."

Casey slipped the rifle to the floorboard and opened his door. Pulling the .32 from his belt, he walked around the rear of the Pontiac. "His name is Martin Wolfe," she said, her voice now uncertain. "He knows everything about the man who hired you, the man who wanted us both dead. He wants to expose this man, to bring him down, to let the world know who and what he is."

As soon as he was at her side again, he pointed the gun at her midsection and motioned toward the river. "Walk."

As they made their way toward the end of the beam from the headlights, she tried once more. "Martin Wolfe is someone you ...."

"I just took care of one cop, and you want me to ...."

"He's not a cop. He's a reporter, and he ...."

She stopped mid-sentence, stepped into the darkness, and swung around. "If you were going to kill me, you would've already done it! You're not going to kill me, so stop playing this game!"

Without warning she lunged at him with a rock in her hand that she must have picked up when he was at the rear of the car. She smashed it against the left side of his head as hard as she could. A bright light flashed through Casey's brain, and he stumbled back, almost falling. He righted himself just in time to stop her next blow with one of his own, a left uppercut under the rib cage that knocked the breath out of her and sent her reeling backward. She fell hard enough to bounce when she hit the ground, rolling down the hill toward the rocky beach of the Tallahatchie River.

The back of her head struck the base of a large rock, just inches from the water, and she wilted. He rushed to her and knelt down to check her breathing. She was unconscious. The back of her head was bleeding.

"I ought to blow your damn brains out!"

Leveling the .32 at the tangled strawberry blonde locks, he imagined the bullet entering her brain, exploding through all that brass and vinegar.

The .32 trembled like the needle in a compass.

Who was he kidding? She was right. If he were going to kill her, he would have already done it. He stood up and put the gun away. Why did he take her with him? She was right about that, too. He didn't know. Something made him do it, maybe the same something that wouldn't let him kill her. He climbed the hill back to the Pontiac.

# CHAPTER 4

A shallow rain began to fall, taking the edge off the heat, but also dampening down the dust on Casey's windshield into a yellow smear that the wipers only made worse. By the time he approached the outskirts of the town of Charleston, the drizzle had become a blinding downpour, making the road little more than a blur.

He fought with the jammed window but water still came through, spraying the side of his face. He pulled out a handkerchief and stuffed it through the opening. The rain forced him down to a crawl along the empty road.

Eventually he spotted a filling station up ahead. It was shut down for the night, but it offered an overhang with a dry spot under it. He pulled over and stopped, leaving the motor running.

Rivers swell quickly in such a torrent, particularly coming off a heavy rain just two days before. She could be under water in a matter of minutes. The arrow on the gas gauge pointed to a little over a quarter tank. He touched his hand lightly against the bruises on his head and shoulder. She had given him her best shot—both times. He had to hand it to Ala Gadomska. The woman packed a wallop. He thought about her lying unconscious among those rocks at the edge of the Tallahatchie.

The rain was falling so hard now pools formed around the Pontiac. It came down in angry sheets, bouncing and streaming off the overhang in all directions. He watched the downpour for several minutes and glanced about, spotting a hand-written sign taped to the glass inside the screen door of the station. With some effort, he made it out.

*Closed. Death in family.*

"Goddamit to hell."

He eased off the clutch and on the gas pedal, and slowly pulled out, turning the steering wheel leftward so that he was soon back on the road but in the westbound lane, following a ribbon of light through a dark and narrow universe where the only other resident may now be just another corpse in a growing line, thanks to a woman in a red dress a thousand miles away.

The farther west the Pontiac traveled, the faster it went, even though the rain refused to relent. Casey bore through it without thinking of anything other than the road, the bridge, and who lay below it. When he reached the

Tallahatchie River, he saw immediately that it had indeed swelled. How badly became clear once he was on the other side. The path between the steel ramp and honeysuckle vines had turned to mud pockmarked with gullies deep enough to break an ankle.

He parked the car, lights on, put on his coat, flipping up the collar, and got out. Twice he slipped making it down the hill, guided as he was only by the headlights. The river's charcoal-colored waters roared below, steadily washing away shoreline.

Soaked through his coat and shirt and into his skin, he rubbed across his eyes repeatedly as he fought to penetrate the darkness alongside the trestlework. He looked for a large rock, but none was there. The water had risen a foot or more above where Ala Gadomska had once lain.

He peered into the river as if she might somehow rise up from the currents, but he knew it was futile. No miracles tonight. When he finally knew it long enough, he stepped sideways to get a look under the trestle. She might have crawled there for safety. It was too black to see anything, and the water prevented him from going farther.

"Hey! Gadomska!" he called out.

He yelled her name a second time, and again no answer. Shaking the rain off his face, he turned to walk back to the Pontiac. A few yards from the car he felt he heard a movement in the thicket to his left, a stirring from something large enough to be a deer, or maybe a human. In the deluge, however, he couldn't be sure he had heard anything at all.

"Gadomska!" he hollered yet again into the night.

The only answer was rain and rushing water and the rumbling from the Pontiac's V8. He remembered the quarter tank of gas, and that was when he gave up on Ala Gadomska, when he told her to go to hell one last time and slogged his way to the car door. Dripping rain, a half-inch of it in his shoes, he shifted into first and glanced up, catching what he thought was a shadow of something in the rearview mirror.

All he could see, however, was streaming water and endless blackness. Soon the rear wheels of the Pontiac were spinning in the mud as he maneuvered to get back onto the road. When the tires finally hit pavement, he had to act fast to stop a sharp spin to the left, straightening the car just in time to get it back facing the bridge. The Tallahatchie River was still under him when he looked in the rearview mirror again and froze.

"What the …!"

In the cracked mirror, hair hanging in her face, clothes smeared with mud, green eyes piercing the rain, was Orella Weicker.

He ground his foot into the brakes, and the car skidded into the rail on the west side of the bridge. Heart pounding, he jumped out and frantically scanned the road. Nothing. He ran into the dark beyond the bridge, but again nothing. He started to cry out, but he had no name for what he'd just seen. So he just stood there on the road, in the rain. Minutes passed before he turned back to the car, no longer able to trust even himself.

Inside the Pontiac Casey wrapped his hands around the steering wheel and beat his forehead against it.

"Have I lost my mind?" he yelled out.

Pushing himself back, he released his grip and dug his fingers through the fake blond hair, pulling and digging, wanting the pain he was causing.

"You fool!" he cried out, and then he grabbed at his neck as if to pull away the rope he'd neatly tied around it.

A chill ran through him as he drove away, and he tried to shake it off. He laughed out loud, at his rattled brain with its crazy notions, the kind of thing you get with a roller-coaster ride through hell. It was nervous, dishonest laughter, and it stopped as soon as he realized he'd busted his left headlight, the perfect excuse for a bored cop to stop him in the night, the perfect reminder of what he had seen, or not seen.

~ ~ ~

The Pontiac needed gas, and he had no choice but to take his chances in Charleston, the last town of any size for dozens of miles. He followed the same road back, passing the closed station where he'd been earlier. He took no notice of it, his mind clouded with thoughts of the bridge and the woman in the rearview mirror.

Close to town the rain finally let up, and it stopped altogether before he pulled into the first open gas station. Next door was a drive-in called *Hank's Hot Dogs* with several cars under its awning. Inside a yellow 1958 Cadillac two teenage girls took their order of hot dogs, fries, and milk shakes from a waitress on skates. A couple empty spots away was a white 1957 Chevrolet Bel Air with a blue light on the roof. He hadn't noticed the blue light from the road. Too late. Casey eased up to the nearest of the two tanks at the Esso station. A neon sign overhead promised that *We Satisfy Our Customers*. Gas was a quarter a gallon.

The jukebox in *Hank's Hot Dogs* was loud. A song with a question. *Who you been lovin' since I been gone?* He knew that song, knew the answer, too. The guy with the red Cadillac and black mustache. "Fill 'er up," he told an attendant in a blue suit after he finally unjammed the car window. "Low test."

A lit cigarette dangled from the corner of the boy's mouth as he coursed his hands over the shiny black pompadour above his thin, chinless face.

"You got it, sir."

The boy hunched his shoulders as a wet gust battled his pomade and blew off the nub of his cigarette. He spit it out.

"Need your tires checked, oil and filter changed? Want me to check your radiator, transmission fluid?"

The busted headlight came to mind, but then so did the cop next door. "Just gas 'er up so I can get the hell out of Dodge."

"Okey-dokey. In a jiffy, sir."

Leaving the motor running as the attendant filled the tank, Casey checked out the Bel Air. The cop had slunk down so far in his seat his chin was even with the dashboard. The muscles in Casey's belly tightened, but nobody at the drive-in was paying attention to the '56 Pontiac gassing up at the Esso. The cop was checking out the teenage girls, and they were giggling to each other between sucks on their straws.

From the Cadillac's radio came *Cathy's Clown*, competing with the music coming out of the jukebox. The blonde in the driver's seat, a Fay Spain look-alike, turned it up, leaned out her window, and called out to the cop. She laughed and tongued her straw as she watched him pull himself upright. The cop was in his mid-thirties, fat with jowls that shook when he poked his head out his window and shouted something back. Fay giggled, played with her straw, turned to her redheaded friend, who nodded.

Soon the Cadillac was pulling out from *Hank's Hot Dogs*, followed closely by the Bel Air, and rolling past Casey onto the stretch toward downtown. The redhead waved to him, and when he didn't wave back, she gave him the finger.

The fog rolled in once he was back on the road, eventually turning so heavy he had to slow the Pontiac to a crawl through the old railroad town of Water Valley. It lifted around Bruce, but then returned in New Houlka and stayed with him through Van Vleet, Okolona, and Amory. The last cloud of it fell away just west of the state line at Gattman, and then it was clear sailing into Alabama.

"To hell with you, Mississippi," Casey said to the rearview mirror. "Kiss my ass goodbye."

A blanket of exhaustion descended on him east of Guin, and he bent over the steering wheel, eyes wide, neck stiff, head and shoulder still sore, humming out loud to keep awake. *Here he comes. That's Cathy's clown.* He needed to think things through, but he was too wiped out to think clearly. He was on Highway 78 now and encountering 18-wheelers in both directions. Their headlights flashed across the highway, reflecting off the pavement. The rain must have drenched Alabama as well as Mississippi.

The more he strained to see, the more those big lights seemed to be coming directly at him. Twice he veered to the right to avoid a truck rounding a curve, catching himself each time when he realized his mind was still playing tricks on him.

The questions about his fix on what was real and what wasn't rattled him. The only choice he had was to trust his instincts, and they were taking him east, direction Phenix City. Duren would come after him. Guys like Duren don't get crossed without repercussions. Casey knew too much. *You've reached a point of no return*, the German had told him. Duren was probably studying his map this very minute. In his green silk robe and bedroom slippers, consulting his partner Tate Kettle.

"'I know where the sonuvabitch is going,'" Casey said out loud, imitating Kettle's drawl. "'He's got it made! He's got five hundred dollars in his pocket and a 1956 Pontiac. He ain't bebopping anywhere but south to Mexico to find him a slick-bellied Juanita to keep him company. I guarantee it.'"

Casey shook his head violently. He was talking to Kettle now, in a loud, angry voice that filled the car. "Guys like you, Tate Kettle, always got it figured out! Always know the score. You the one who explains the natives to Duren, right?"

And Duren? "The Big Mahah. You so smart you're going to get on the phone to Jackson and New Orleans and tell 'em to be on the lookout, right? Neither one of you figure I'll go straight to Phenix City. You too smart to think I'd go right back to Clyde Point!" Duren, like Kettle, was in the Pontiac with him. "I don't like to get crossed either. I got some settling to do with my friend Clyde Point. Don't I, Clyde?"

Clyde had entered the Pontiac, too.

Spitting onto the floorboard the gall that had formed in his mouth, he went over the scene in which Clyde pitched the deal, played him for the sucker he was. He searched through it, looking for a sign, for anything that might have tipped him off.

In his mind, he watched Clyde once again from across the table at his roadhouse in Phenix City, forking his steak, sopping up the juices with a fistful of bread. He was a noisy eater, Clyde Point, snorting, grunting, wiping his hand across the cloth napkin stuck in his collar. On the wall behind him hung a pinup calendar with July's model, a naked, long-legged, raven-haired beauty in front of a waterfall.

*Got me a fugitive here at the table. Wanted dead or alive. Murder first degree. His own cousin, a family man with connections. Mmmm-mmm. Do have some good news for you. Betcha didn't know your gal in Jonesboro got the stolen vehicle charge dropped.*

Clyde loved impressing people with what he knew and they didn't. He must have loved the dumb, confused look on Casey's face that night in the Dixie Inn.

Deep in the woods several miles from Phenix City, it was the last whorehouse in what used to be Sin City USA. The air was thick with the smells of frying fish, pulled pork barbecue, whiskey, cheap perfume, rutting soldiers, and Clyde's bragging. He had turned the place around for Ike Berliner. Ike couldn't do without him. Ike whose real name is Albrecht, German, but figures Ike is more patriotic. Ike the pussy hound who gets first crack at every woman he hires or she doesn't get hired.

*How do you know she got the charge dropped?*

*I told her to. I called her up, told her you had plenty enough against you without it, and she was too scared not to do it. Still going to that juke joint to get her jollies, though. Woman's crazy. Got to have it. We have a couple here like that. They'd work for free if we weren't so generous.*

Clyde was a liar but why would he lie about Orella? He did know her. Casey introduced him. He had been in Jonesboro around the time it all happened, promising Casey a job down in Alabama. That's how Casey got his number.

71

"You delivered on that IOU, didn't you, you sonuvabitch?" Casey told Clyde, the only one left with him in the car.

The pool sharks talk about getting position, putting the other guy in the right spot to take him out. That was the talk about Orella. The job came up next, just before Joe Arles, Clyde's man Friday, peeked his head in the door. A gold medallion with the face of an Axtec sun hung from Arles' bull neck. *Mr. Berliner's ready to see you.*

Clyde dropped his fork and stood up. *Look, no time to explain. Ike wants to know, and I have to tell him. We got a job for you. A big job. You want it or not? This is your IOU. Your last chance, too. What's your answer?*

"Tell Ike and your Big Mahah that Casey Eubanks is taking the job, whatever the hell it is," Casey said, repeating his answer that night word for word, only this time louder and harder, like a sucker does after he realizes what the deal really was and he never had a clue.

~ ~ ~

The mountains just west of Birmingham loomed over the Pontiac like a silent tribunal. Shoulders stooped, black-robed against the sky, they watched and deliberated as Casey followed the highway into Jones Valley and the heart of the city. He was too tired to figure out a detour. The streets were lit up like Macy's at Christmas, but they were empty.

Everywhere was the odor of burnt fuel. The air was dry and grainy. Soot formed on the Pontiac's windshield

72

as he drove from block to block. It seemed to cover everything—the shrubs along the sidewalks, park benches, phone booths, the tops of trashcans. Casey could even taste it, the grind and gristle of Bombingham. Three in the morning, and the city looked like the Martians had come and vaporized the people.

Casey passed locked-up pawnshops, the darkened vestibules of movie palaces where *Dinosaurus* and *The Crimson Kimono* had played just before the Martians did their work. He drove by union halls and corner bars, all dark and empty with not even a whore or bum in the alleyways. Birmingham had shut down, no traffic, no life, making the Pontiac a one-eyed sitting duck for street after empty street.

At every corner, Casey's stomach knotted up for the cop who was never there. A couple times he thought he saw the bumper or fender of a patrol car at the intersection of a parallel street, but he wasn't sure. The town was dead, dead like Baby Face, dead like Ala Gadomska.

The deeper he drove into it the more he felt like the last human on earth.

Then, at the next turn, he saw that he wasn't alone in Birmingham. Three cop cars, their lights flashing, had stopped and pulled alongside a Lincoln Continental. On the street, officers surrounded a young black man in a white suit, white fedora, and pink shirt. The man looked straight ahead as the officers fired questions at him. Casey had no choice but to drive past them, and he caught the attention of one of the cops as he did. The officer motioned for him to pull over.

Then, his hand patting his holstered gun, the cop left the gathering and ambled toward the Pontiac. He was tall and lean, his mouth a straight line, his eyes hidden under his cap. Casey kicked the rifle under the seat as best he could—cursing himself for leaving it on the floorboard-- and rolled the window down. He sat up tall to try to hide the bruise Ala Gadomska had given him. When the cop reached the car, he leaned against the window and bent down to peer inside. A scar ran from cheek to jaw line to just above the man's Adam's apple, obviously the work of a carving knife big enough to take someone's head off. On the back of his right hand was a small tattoo of the Southern Cross.

"Identification, sir."

Casey pulled out the driver's license and handed it to him. The officer studied it closely, turning it from side to side.

"Something wrong?"

The officer's eyes shifted to Casey as he handed the license back to him. "Got a headlight out, Mr. Thompson. Need to get that fixed."

"You're right. Hadn't had a chance to …."

"What you do for a living, Mr. Thompson?"

"I'm a salesman."

"What do you sell?"

"Burial insurance."

"What are you doing on these streets this time of night?"

"Just traveling through, heading south."

The cop motioned toward the black man, who was now being ushered into one of the patrol cars. "See that young fella over there. He's a preacher, a troublemaker, been stirring up a lot of folks. Thinks it's his God-given right to sit next to white people at a lunch counter. What you think about that?"

Casey shrugged.

"You know what our police commissioner says about his type? Says go after 'em with a Confederate flag in one hand and a gun in the other."

"What'd he do?"

"It's three in the morning, and he's dressed to kill. We're going to find out."

The cop smiled and then slapped the roof of the car. "Ought to be plenty customers for your line of work, Mr. Thompson. Let us know if we can help you find some. And get that light taken care of."

Casey pulled away. He knew about this city, had read about it in the papers, seen it on the television. On a deserted street a couple blocks away, he pulled over and put the rifle in the trunk.

"To hell with your troublemakers," he said, getting back in and slamming the door shut, "and to hell with your police commissioner, too."

Eventually the city and the rust-red plumes rising from the smoke stacks on Red Mountain were behind him.

So was a tractor trailer rig bellowing for him to get going or get out of the way. He realized he'd slowed to forty miles an hour. As he moved to the right, the Mack driver passed him mouthing some obscenity. Casey gave him an empty-eyed glance and turned back to the road.

He tried to shake off the close call he'd just had in Birmingham. One wrong move, and he would've pulled the .32 from his pocket, killed his second cop, and then be dead himself before the parked Lincoln had slipped from his rearview mirror. The cop with the tattoo never bothered to check beyond the fake license. All he cared about was the preacher in the white suit. The preacher was the real danger.

Soon it was the fog in his head that Casey was trying to shake. He had to fight just to keep his eyes from glazing over like some drunk on a bender. A pot of black coffee would fix everything, but nothing was open. He drove and kept driving until his eyes finally slid shut and he found himself faraway in a black forest, on his feet, gliding across black ice toward a distant shore line. He couldn't see his legs, and his hands grappled with a spinning wheel suspended in midair, and he wondered how he got into this situation.

A jolting thump and loud groan from the Pontiac's shock absorbers pushed him out of his dream into a shadowy cylinder of road, ditch, bush and gravel. He struggled to get his brain and feet coordinated, and the brakes finally kicked in, just shy of a fence post.

The near crash had cleared the fog in his head but also shoved his face against the steering wheel, busting the inside of his upper lip. Blood pooled in his mouth, and he pulled back to spit it out. In the Pontiac's headlight was a chicken wire mesh just inches from the hood. The fence stretched into the shadows to either side, and it was held up by iron posts leaning toward one another. One sagged nearly to the ground.

Behind the chicken wire was a weatherworn army of saints, angels, and Romans—a St. Francis in his cassock with a bird on his shoulder, an angel at the rim of a birdbath, one of its wings missing, a bust of Caesar in a wheelbarrow. Scattered among them were plows, pumps, singletrees, and doubletrees, everything rusted out and worthless. The first light was coming over the horizon, and Casey could make out the silhouette of a tin-roofed dogtrot beyond the junk pile. It had an end-to-end porch and unlit windows with the shades drawn. On the porch, just to the right of the front door, was a Coca-Cola cooler with ICE COLD emblazoned on it in giant white letters.

Something moved in the shadows, and he stepped out to get a better look. The 350 motor rumbled on. He wasn't the only breathing creature within earshot of it. The moment he took a step forward, a growl came out of the darkness just below the busted left headlight. With it came a rancid smell. Before Casey could connect smell and growl, a black-tongued monster lunged up at the fence, teeth bared, drool dangling from both corners of its mouth. Chicken wire would never hold such a dog, even if the fence posts were firm. Casey reached for the .32 and stepped back behind the door of the Pontiac.

That same moment, the dog lunged again and this time crashed through the fence, its shoulder hitting the left side of the car's front grill like a tackle barreling into a stalled halfback. Casey jumped into the driver's seat just as the dog slammed against the door. Lights came on inside the dogtrot.

Grabbing the gearshift, he shoved it into reverse and hit the gas, popping rocks in every direction as the dog slid down onto the gravel. Shifting to first, he spun the steering wheel hard to the left and then to the right, pumping the accelerator, and careened out of the lot and back onto the highway with the dog racing behind him, its bay piercing the night.

Casey didn't breath until he was a hundred yards down the road and checking in the rearview mirror. The animal was still running straight down the white line hell-bent to catch the '56 Pontiac and the trespasser driving it.

He didn't look in the mirror again for the rest of the trip down Highway 280 to Phenix City, even when he stopped to gas up. It was early morning when he crossed the Georgia Central railroad tracks on the outskirts of town. He looked for a motel although he wondered if he'd actually be able to sleep, whether he was beyond sleep. He had to try. Without sleep he'd never come up with a plan. He couldn't just walk into Ike Berliner's place like John Wayne and start shooting. For once in his life, he needed to be smart.

Just off Opelika Road he found Sleepy's. A neon Disney dwarf with a long beard and a wagon full of gems presided over the place from his perch on the roof. After parking the Pontiac between a Chevrolet Biscayne station wagon and a Ford Ranchero, Casey buttoned his coat up to cover as best he could the blood stains on his shirt. His clothes were still wet.

The brunette behind the desk eased the phone back down on the receiver when she saw him at the door of the lobby. Plucking a well-chewed pencil out of her mouth, she leaned across the counter and smiled under her dark-rimmed glasses. From the door, the glasses made her look like a teenaged librarian, but the closer he got the more she looked like a character out of one of those books the libraries ban. The top buttons of her white blouse were loose, putting on display the ruby drop necklace hanging from her neck as well as the rise of her pert breasts.

"What can I do for you, handsome?" she asked him, resting her head on her palm and slipping her pencil in and out of her mouth as she waited for his answer. The class ring on her finger said *1959*. A wad of wax beneath the blue stone kept it from falling off.

Casey studied her as she slowly pulled the pencil out from deep inside her mouth and puckered around the void that it left.

"Just a room, kiddo," he told her. "That's all I need. Just a room."

The pucker turned sad as she pulled out a ledger and handed him a form to fill out. "Tired cowboy, huh?" she said, watching him sign the name "Marcel Camp" on the ledger. Then looking up past his shoulder to the Pontiac outside: "That's a '56, ain't it, Mr. Camp?"

He ignored the question, although he liked hearing her call him Mr. Camp. Marcel Camp was one of the great pool sharks of all time even if this bimbo never heard of him. He took the keys from her.

"Room 212, second floor, up the stairs. Sleep tight."

He walked out the door to park the car around back.

"What's happened to desk clerks?" he asked himself. "They all turned cocksucker?"

The rear parking lot was empty, but he left the rifle in the trunk. No use risking someone spotting him from a motel window. The .32 in his inside pocket would do if he needed it. He walked up the outside stairway to the second floor. His room was just past the corner. The curtains were pulled back.

Room service hadn't gotten to 212 yet. The bed was unmade, and cigarette butts filled the ashtray on the table next to it. He pulled off the sheets and threw them in a corner.

After closing the curtains, he hung his coat on a bedpost and stretched out across the mattress. It wasn't long before he was in a shallow, fitful sleep, the kind of no-rest sleep he'd had ever since he'd been on the run.

Soon he was twisting and twitching, grabbing air around him, trying to get a grip on the steering wheel. The wheel was spinning out of control, and he couldn't for the life of him understand why he didn't plunge into the black void around him. Maybe he already had, because in the void was a mirror and he was staring into it, not at himself but at what was behind him. He got so close he could feel the cold glass against his cheek, so close he finally saw her, in the rain, her clothes soaked, her hair in her face, her lips shaping soundless words. The longer he stared, the more confused he became.

Something wasn't right. It was her face. Her face was wrong. His eyelashes touched the glass. He couldn't turn to see the woman behind him. He only had the mirror, and he wanted to enter it, to reach into it and reach her before something happened to her. Yet he wasn't even sure who the woman was, whether she was Ala Gadomska, Orella, or some other woman standing there in the rain in the middle of the road.

He tried to speak but couldn't, as if he had been stricken mute. In his forced silence, he heard someone beating on the car window next to him, and he saw it was her, only inches away yet her face still obscure. The beating grew louder and louder, and a voice called to him, but it was raspy and demanding, a man's voice.

"Eubanks! Eubanks!"

Casey jumped up from the bed to a sitting position, his heart thumping, the woman in the window slipping back into the void.

"Casey Eubanks," the voice shouted again from the balcony outside.

Casey reached for his coat and grabbed the .32. Wiping his eyes with the back of his hand, he swung his legs onto the floor and stumbled to the door.

"I hear you in there, Eubanks. Open the damn door. It's Martin Wolfe. Open this door and save your rotten life."

Martin Wolfe. It took a minute, but then he remembered. Ala Gadomska's reporter friend, the name she mentioned at the river, the man she said could help him. Casey shook the dream out of his head and cracked the door, his gun ready. On the other side stood a short, heavy-set man in a rumpled brown suit, catfish smile stretched across his broad face, eyes lit up like tiny searchlights and bearing down on Casey.

Casey weighed whether to slam the door in his face or let him in. He decided to chance it and backed away slowly with his gun trained on the man's chest.

"You better have a helluva story, all I got to say."

Wolfe walked in, giving Casey a sideways once-over. A bouquet of Ole Spice and cigarettes accompanied him. Ignoring the gun pointed at him, he pushed his fedora to the back of his head, loosened his polka-dotted tie, and pulled at the unbuttoned collar of his shirt. When he reached into his coat pocket, Casey yelled, "Hey!"

Wolfe waved his forefinger and slowly pulled out a pack of Lucky Strikes. Casey watched as he shook one out of the pack and stuck it in his mouth. From another pocket came a wooden poker chip, quickly replaced by a pack of matches.

"Would offer you one, but you not much of a smoker, as I recall."

The drawl tended to bury last letters.

"How do you know what I do or don't do? And who the hell you say you are?"

The man lit his cigarette and fished again in his pockets. Wincing at a wisp of smoke that drifted into his eye, he handed Casey a card that read.


*Martin Wolfe*
*Freelance Writer*
*Memphis, Tenn.*
*6-9653*


"What am I supposed to do with this?"

Casey crumpled the card in his fist and tossed it on the bed.

"You don't look so good, Eubanks. "Course, you goin' be looking dead if you don't get your stuff and leave with me right now."

"What are you talking about?"

"You got maybe another five, ten minutes before Ike Berliner's goons show up, and I'm your only ticket out of here."

The reporter walked to the corner of the window and peered behind the closed curtain at the parking lot below.

"You're pretty predictable, you know. I figured you'd be heading this way to get even with Clyde, and I'll bet Ike did, too. We all been waiting for the curly blond in the '56 Pontiac." He stopped and grinned, exposing a missing eyetooth.

"Ike's problem is his sources talk to me, too."

Casey took a long look at Wolfe, remembering what Ala Gadomska had said. *He knows everything about the man who hired you. He wants to expose this man, to bring him down.* He noticed a thin chain around Wolfe's neck under his loosened tie. Casey lowered the .32.

"You met Lucy, little gal downstairs. One of Ike's girls." Wolfe stopped for a private thought. "Lordy. Got a ring from last year's star quarterback at the local high school. Took just one steamy night at the Dixie Inn. Got a nice ruby necklace from Ike. Also available for lonely travelers, by the way."

"You got a point with all this?"

Wolfe stepped away from the curtain and faced Casey.

"Yes, I certainly do. Ike Berliner doesn't know it, but Lucy's on my tab, too. I had her on the lookout. That's why I'm here. I made her guarantee she'd call me first, although I'm worried she didn't wait long enough to make that second phone call."

Casey laid the gun on the bed.

"What about Clyde Point?"

Wolfe sighed. "I'm kind of worried about Clyde's health."

"What do you mean?"

"I mean ol' Clyde got an unfriendly escort out of his roadhouse last night."

84

Casey stared at him. "How do you know that?"

"Look, we really don't have time to palaver. My good friends keep me in the know, okay? Once word got out about what happened …. uh, I mean what didn't happen in Mississippi, Clyde's stock in the company took a nosedive." A cloud fell across Wolfe's face. "These boys don't play around. And they don't waste time either. You should know …"

The sound of a car pulling into the lot stopped him mid-sentence. Both turned to the window and saw a late model Impala park alongside Casey's Pontiac. Men immediately poured out.

"Time to skedaddle," Wolfe told him, tossing his cigarette as he opened the door. "I'm parked at the next building. Just follow me."

Casey didn't argue. Snatching his coat, he followed Wolfe, grabbing his gun and the crumpled card off the bed before shutting the door behind him. They hurried along the balcony in the opposite direction from the parking lot and down a stairway at the far end of the building.

By the time they reached the bottom of the stairs, they could hear commotion on the second floor. When they stepped out onto the side lot that the motel shared with a neighboring garage, a hood with a bad case of acne welcomed them with a German Luger at point-blank range. Before Casey could even react, Wolfe had the kid floored with a roundhouse left that came out of nowhere. They made it to his Studebaker with the sound of pounding feet on the metal balcony ringing in their ears.

# CHAPTER 5

A 10-year-old maroon Studebaker that smelled like Martin Wolfe waited for them in the parking lot next to Sleepy's. On the dashboard by the steering wheel was a paper cup with a swallow or two of coffee still in it. Wolfe threw the cup out as he jumped into the driver seat and revved up the motor. The pounding feet they'd heard along the balcony were now rushing down the stairs and onto the lot.

Wolfe left a stretch of tire marks as he spun off onto Holland Drive, where they just missed a milk truck making its morning rounds. Gunning the Studebaker across the railroad tracks, he zigzagged through Phenix City's back neighborhoods, barely missing several trashcans and one transfixed cocker spaniel but bumping a kid's red wagon down a steep ditch by the road.

Neither man spoke a word but every few seconds Wolfe checked the rear view mirror and Casey the side mirror. Just before crossing the Chattahoochee River, the Impala came into view, barreling down a narrow side street two blocks away that merged into theirs. Soon they heard back-to-back popping sounds, and bullets whizzed past them toward some unknown destination.

"Told you they mean business," Wolfe said with a quick sideways glance.

Once in Columbus, he veered south, then east a block later before turning again, this time north to Talbotton Road, which took him northeast past the college and the golf course. The Impala was nowhere in sight.

"Berliner's boys don't know this side of the tracks. They're all toughs from someplace else, and what they know is busting heads and shaking down GIs."

"What about my car?"

"Your car? You mean Max Duren's car. What do you think they told little Lucy to look for?"

Rows of white-framed mill houses, each one identical to the other, swept past them, each with the same narrow porch and patch of yard. Here and there was an overturned tricycle or forgotten doll. They drove past the body shops and hamburger joints that bordered the mill houses, then past the strip malls at the edge of town.

Eventually Columbus and Phenix City were behind them, and the nose of the Studebaker pointed toward Atlanta, a hundred miles northeast. Still no sign of the Impala. Casey was impressed.

Leaning back in his seat for the first time since they got in the car, Wolfe pulled another Lucky out of his shirt pocket and waved it at Casey, who shook his head.

"That's right. Not a smoker. Nearly forgot."

Casey shrugged.

Wolfe lit the cigarette for himself.

"How the hell you survive?"

"How the hell you know I don't smoke?"

Wolfe smiled. "I know which shoe you put on first in the morning, you sonuvabitch. What the hell you think?"

He held the cigarette in the air, pondering it a moment, and then popped it between his lips. "Damned cancer sticks going to kill me some day." He dragged deeply and blew a smoke ring. "That is, if hanging out with you doesn't first."

Casey surveyed his surroundings. In the backseat were scattered piles of newspapers, jazz magazines, a couple crime novels, a book of poetry, file folders thick with papers, and several notepads filled with what was apparently Wolfe's chicken scratch. In the corner was a record album that looked brand new, *Mingus Dynasty*. A couple empty coke bottles and more newspapers were on the back floorboard. In front, the butts of a half-dozen Lucky Strikes were in the ashtray.

"You live in this heap?"

Wolfe chuckled. "Me and the Studebaker been through a lot together."

Casey shifted, looked away, flinched when he caught sight of a cop car parked at the *Breakfast Palace*.

"So what now? You save my ass so you can turn me in to the cops?"

The Lucky bobbed in Wolfe's mouth as he answered. "Naw. You better stay with me a bit. It'd serve you right, though, after leaving my late wife's niece back at that godforsaken Mississippi sinkhole to be supper for the rats and snakes."

Casey turned from the window to the round-faced reporter but said nothing.

Wolfe nodded meaningfully.

"Yeah, that's right. Ala Gadomska."

"Who and what the hell are you talking about?"

"Ala called me early this morning after walking through rain, fog, mud, and a pack of mangy strays to get to a phone. Hey, that's a nasty cut you got side of your head."

"She called you?" Casey ignored the crack about the cut.

"Who she gonna call? The local police chief? She gave you some good advice, but you wouldn't listen. You're in way over your head, Eubanks. You're dealing with a network that stretches from Richmond to New Orleans, and they got your number, buddy."

Casey rubbed his chest, moved his fingers close enough to feel the .32. He figured he'd be using it soon. "Seems like everybody's got my number."

"Yeah, good thing you didn't do what you were paid to do back in Mississippi. Otherwise, I'd have you in *my* crosshairs. She's family. Look, Casey Eubanks, I know all about you. Friend of mine saw Clyde drop you off at the station in Columbus. Watched you myself climb on that Greyhound to Memphis.

"I knew Clyde sent you on a mission. Just didn't know what. Was all I could do not to introduce myself to you then and there in that bus station, but I figured the time wasn't right. Nearly cost my niece her life. I warned her, though, told her to be on the lookout, that something was up. She's as stubborn as her aunt was. Eubanks, these guys set you up to kill Ala, then they were going to kill you and brag to the world about it. That's what these guys do. They get hillbillies and Kluxers, small-timers like you, to do their dirty work for them, and do it for little or nothing. They got plenty of money but they're as cheap with their hirelings as they are with their lintheads and their field hands.

"What kind of weapon they give you to kill Ala? She didn't tell me, but I'll bet it was a shotgun, an old shotgun or a ten dollar rifle. Think Max Duren can't afford a high-powered, top-of-the-line rifle for his paid hitman? Hellfire. Your main purpose was to scare the shit out of everybody, whether you killed Ala or not. They were taking you out regardless and getting back whatever money they gave you. Well, you surprised the hell out of 'em. They figured you'd at least shoot the woman. Instead you shoot the cop they planted. That little miscalculation may have cost your friend Clyde his life.

"You've got their attention now, Casey Eubanks. I think you even have them scared, and that's not a very healthy thing to do. After all, you met Max Duren in person. You received a rare opportunity. He's the original invisible man. I'm not surprised, though. If I know Max Duren at all, he got a very special pleasure out of interviewing a dead man. That must have delighted him to no end, the sweet little trick they were about to play on you. Yes, yes, you met Max, Tate Kettle. You even got to talk with my good buddy Monte."

Casey met the gap-toothed grin with a look of disgust. "You sure know a lot of cocksuckers. And dammit how you know who I supposedly met in Memphis?"

Wolfe beamed. "I told you I have good sources. Remember Rosie, the aging doll with the copper-colored hair?" Casey shook his head. "The waitress at the Peabody. I got a network, too. Look, you're important to Duren's crowd now. They can't have you crisscrossing the South running your mouth. They got to take care of you before you talk to people like me. They don't worry about the law because they own the law. They don't own me."

"So Mr. Writer's gonna save me by telling the world my problems."

Wolfe pulled his tie off and further loosened the collar around his ample neck. The chain caught Casey's attention again. He reached over and plucked at it.

"What's the jewelry?"

Wolfe pulled the chain out from under his collar. At the end hung a wooden medallion featuring a man in a long robe cupping a set of carpenter tools in his apron. "St. Joe, the working stiff saint."

"Believe in voodoo, huh?

"Better'n kissin' rattlesnakes. Hey, maybe I shoulda had tattoos done instead, huh?"

The look on Casey's face inspired a follow up. "Tell me about those markings of yours. Gilda, right? Ah, what a woman."

"Gilda" caught him off guard. The man even knows about his tattoos. No use to protest or pretend. They were Casey's pride, the Rita on each arm, in her silk nightie, her long hair flowing down onto her bare shoulders, feet tucked under her bottom, hands on her knees, curves everywhere.

"Got 'em in a little parlor outside Fort Bragg. Fella was a real artist." He rubbed his arms instinctively and muttered under his breath, "Only woman never betrayed me."

Wolfe pulled deep on his cigarette before stubbing it out. "Oh, she'd betray you. Soon as the wrong fella spots 'em. Man with tattoos like yours, easy to remember. Still, what you're trying to say is not true. Not true. I met your woman up in North Carolina, but more on that later. You got cops chasing you, Max Duren and Ike Berliner chasing you, a couple of dead bodies, including one of Spider Creek, Mississippi's finest. What do you do to help somebody in a situation like that? Good thing for you is I'm the only one this side of the law who's connected those dead bodies."

"You met Orella?"

"I'll get to that."

Wolfe glanced at Casey, lips pursed.

"I made that connection because I'm a reporter, a damned good one, and I've been following a story that's a lot bigger than you, but you're definitely part of that story, you and the Love Goddess under your sleeves. Soon as I heard a tattooed friend of Clyde's had showed up at the Dixie Inn, I thought to myself, `Lordy, lordy.'"

"You just a smart fella. Know everybody and everything. The truth is, the whole damned world knows about me. Knows I killed Bux Baggett, stole Orella Weicker's car, ran off to Myrtle Beach, Phenix City, and pretty soon it'll know the rest."

"World doesn't know about Myrtle Beach."

Another surprise. "Of course it does. Gin Smith told the world."

"Who?"

"Orella's gin-soaked brother. The ex-cop. Knew I was hiding out in Myrtle Beach. She figured that's where I'd go, and she sent him. We'd been there once, the two of us, and she knew I liked it. So he finds me, and I take off to Phenix City. None of this is news to a genius like you."

"Yep, she told me. But neither she nor Gin told another soul, including the cops. Like I said, it's Orella, not your Gilda, who never betrayed you. She even had the stolen car charge against you dropped."

"Yeah, after Clyde Point told her to."

"Give me a break. Since when does Orella Weicker do what Clyde Point tells her to do? She got that charge dropped because she loves you despite everything."

93

"Say everything you say is true, why in the hell should I trust you?"

Wolfe shook his head. "You sittin' in this car talkin' to me, aren't you? Instead of riding in the trunk of a new Impala with a third eye just above the other two."

Casey fell silent.

Wolfe let him ponder for a few moments all that had been said. "Casey, it's true, all I have is a pen. You're right. But with that pen I can put those doublecrossin' goosesteppers on the front page of America, and that ain't half bad."

"You'd do that for me, huh? Right out of the goodness of your heart. You're a heck of a fellow, ain't you."

"Do it for you?" Wolfe snorted. "I've been chasing that sonuvabitch Duren for twenty years. I'm doing it for my own damn self, and if it gets him off your back, well, so much the better. Don't kid yourself. You may spend some time behind bars, but it's better than where Duren's bunch wants to put you. As for me, I happen to think you have some mitigating circumstances in your case. If you work with us, we'll see …"

"What do you mean 'us'?"

"I mean I'm not alone on this. I have a friend who's in a position to help you a lot more than me. With a little luck—something you've been short of lately—he might even save you from a lifetime in jail. What we need is your story, all of it, and every damned word on the record."

"Let's pretend I'm listening."

94

Wolfe folded his hands over the steering wheel. Eyes fixed on the road, grin gone, he was a man making his big pitch, taking the one shot, bull's-eye or nothing.

"Clyde Point is a greedy and ambitious lieutenant in this outfit, desperate to move up the line, to impress the bosses. We were watching him long before he got to Phenix City. He's been a point man for them, making contacts, setting up businesses. He was hoping to get something going in your town, his old stomping grounds.

"That's how I found out about you, how I met Orella Weicker. She's quite a woman, a good woman no matter what you might think. Clyde's a link into the network that we thought we could tap. This is a network that includes politicians, judges, publishers, preachers, big farmers like Tate Kettle, the businessmen who run this holy backwater called the South. They don't like colored people who stray out of their place. Keep 'em in rags, likes those boys over there."

He nodded toward a band of black youths crossing a field of still-green cotton, a half-dozen or them, all sizes and shapes, one as young as six or eight, a couple of them six-feet-tall teenagers, shirtless and shoeless in tattered jeans and overalls, carrying reed fishing poles, buckets and bait baskets. Dragging up the rear was a boy so badly deformed he walked crablike, with his right leg stretched in front, bent at the knee, and his torso bent back over his left. He used the left leg to push himself forward while a stick helped him keep balance. The rest would stop every now and then to let him catch up. They walked in the direction of a creek that ran under the highway ahead and cut across the length of the field to a stand of trees in the distance.

"And what they sure as hell don't like are Yankee organizers stirring up their field hands. Kettle was Duren's ticket, first into the Memphis inner circle, then into the Federation. That's what it calls itself, the Federation. Duren was a perfect fit, a real deal, old-line Nazi from Deutschland with a stash of cash dating back to the war and international connections to boot. That made him a hero to these cornpone versions. Kettle helped get Duren set up—strip clubs, gambling joints, farms and timberland, and then the chain of Bengal mills that the ITU has targeted."

Casey was listening. "The what?"

"The ITU, International Textiles Union, the one Ala works for. They've got their sights on plants in Mississippi, Alabama, Georgia. Ala was the one tipped me off about the mysterious German in the duck's nest at the Peabody. She even told me about Berliner."

"What about Berliner?"

"Berliner's German, too, but he's a Lodz German from an old textiles family in Poland. *Red Lodz*, big factory town, lots of smokestacks, all Communist now. Ala came from Lodz. So did my wife. Small world, huh?"

"Your late wife?"

"Yep. Died in 1950. Cancer. Eaten up with it."

Wolfe lit another cigarette. "Berliner's been in the States a long time, served as a contact for the Nazi ring

96

over here during the war. With his family history, we're sure he's been an adviser, probably silent partner, in Duren's Bengal holdings, but his heart and soul are in women and gambling. As for Duren and Kettle, what they care about are money and power. Know what John D. Rockefeller once said? `God gave me my money. The power to make money is a gift from God.' He had his kingdom, and these fellows got theirs. Oh, yeah, they talk about the niggers and the Jews and the communists and the Polacks and the Yankees and the trouble-making reporters like me. What they're really saying is the kingdom is theirs, and no one threatens the kingdom."

A wisp of smoke from the Lucky drifted about Wolfe's head. "You read about Eichmann, the Nazi who got caught in Argentina back in May, all that business about taking him to Israel and having him tried."

Despite Casey's blank look, Wolfe continued. "Eichmann's capture got people thinking who else might be out there. Lots of other fish swimming around in those waters. Max Duren is one of 'em. I've been tracking this guy off and on since the early Forties. All the way to South America. You probably never heard of Fritz Duquesne. He was a German spy on the New York docks, working with the maritime's' union, of all things. Duren was part of his gang and later with another called the Werewolf. Duquesne eventually got caught. Duren got away. Of course, his name back then was Alois Dürren.

"So who's this person you're working with?"

"A man I've known since those days in South America. We were down there for the same reason. He listens to me when I make a case for someone, which is what I'm doing for you. If you play your cards right, he might can get you into what they call the `protected informant' program. You give us information, and we give you protection."

"Who's this guy with?"

Casey waited for an answer.

"The FBI."

Casey turned back to the highway, reached into his coat pocket and pulled out the .32. "Take that farm road down there," he ordered.

Wolfe, seeing his one shot miss, slowed and took the turn without protest. The rutted dirt road, narrowed by bramble bush on both sides, led to a clearing where a decrepit shack sat off to the right. Wolfe pulled in front of it. As the motor idled, a dog stepped out from the side of the shack and slowly climbed the steps onto its porch. A mix of beagle and Jack Russell, with ribs showing and patches of hair missing, it rested on its haunches to study the proceedings in the Studebaker.

"Casey . . ."

"So this big plan of yours is to turn me over to the FBI."

"You'd only be dealing with him and me. J. Edgar has not blessed this operation. He doesn't even know about it. My friend is a straight-up guy who won't give his word if he can't keep it." Wolfe waved a finger at the gun in Casey's hand. "That's a .32, isn't it?"

"Enough to take care of things."

The gun in his face, Wolfe resumed. "The South is about to blow wide open. These lunch-counter sit-ins are just the first cracks in the fortress wall. When Mack Parker got lynched over in Mississippi last year, they didn't even return an indictment, but it stirred up a hornet's nest in Washington, and Kettle & Company paid attention. They're on edge. The river bottoms down here are full of the bodies of negroes who didn't know their place, and more than a few labor organizers, too. Add to that this Eichmann business, the possibility that Kennedy might win this fall, and now union trouble. These boys are digging in their heels, bound and determined to hold onto what they've got, come hell or high water. They're not going to let some pool hustler from North Carolina put a spotlight on their dealings. You got a lot stacked against you, Casey. For all your sins, you need someone on your side."

The air hung heavy between them.

"And your job is to write about it in the *Saturday Evening Post*, right?"

"Well, not quite. It's a magazine out of Chicago, called *Labor*."

"Never heard of it."

"You will when this story comes out. Lots of people will."

The dog whimpered and slipped onto the ground in front of the porch. It was shaking.

"Get out of the car, Mr. Writer."

"Casey, I'm the only friend you got in this world. Sad as that may be, it's true. I'm on the level, and you know I am. Where you gonna go now? You got no way out."

The .32 motioned him toward the door. Wolfe reached for the keys in the ignition but then, like a lawyer making his closing argument:

"I was at Remagen, Battle of the Bulge. I know the difference between a cold-blooded murderer and someone who killed because he thought he had to. You plugged a crooked cop before he could plug you. As for your cousin Bux, well, I'm working on a hunch I'm not ready to discuss yet. For damn sure, you're no saint, Casey Eubanks, but you're no murderer either. Orella Weicker told me that herself, and she was right. If you were, Ala would be dead now."

"Get out of the car before I show you just how easy it is for me to pull this trigger."

Wolfe killed the motor, leaving the keys, and climbed out. He stepped a couple of feet away from the door as Casey slid over to the driver's seat with the gun still pointed at the reporter. The dog let loose a short, sharp, impatient yelp.

Wolfe gave it a quick assessment. "You're like that fyce over there. Lost, no place to go, in bad need of a friend. You're not going to shoot me. Who you trying to kid?" He probed Casey's eyes. "But, hell, even I respect a loaded gun. For all I know, you might aim above my head and shoot me by accident. That'd be a hell of a note, wouldn't it?"

"You expect me to sign on with you and this friend of yours. I don't know you, and you don't know me. What the hell do you think I am? None of you know the first thing about me. Not you or that Polack bitch or Berliner or that Big Mahah Duren. Maybe I should air condition that belly of yours."

Wolfe reached into his coat pocket and pulled out the poker chip Casey had noticed earlier. He ran his thumb across it and began rolling it across his knuckles. "`Be kind,' the philosopher said, `for everyone you meet is fighting a great battle.'"

Casey fired the engine, slipped it into gear, and stopped to study the forlorn reporter and the dog inching toward him cautiously.

"What's with the poker chip? Another good luck charm?"

"It's a wooden nickel. Something my daddy gave me when I was a little boy. Told me never to take another one."

As the Studebaker eased back onto the dirt road toward the highway, Casey glanced at Wolfe one more time. Mr. Writer was kneeling down, petting the fyce, checking his watch.

~ ~ ~

The blues came over Casey north of Warm Springs as he passed through piney woods and cattle farm country.

He was traveling north toward Atlanta but not sure why or what his destination was. He wasn't sure if he was running from or toward the people chasing him.

*Lost, no place to go, in bad need of a friend.*

He knew no one in Atlanta or for a hundred miles in any direction from Atlanta.

Martin Wolfe's voice was still in his head, and the man was in his nostrils, too—the cigarette butts and coffee stains, the stink of living one's life in a ten-year-old car. For the first time he noticed a ragged-edged paperback near the gas pedal. *Neon Wilderness*. Casey kicked it away.

On a hunch he reached under the driver's seat. A good hunch. Out from under came a pint of Jack Daniel's Black. Only a couple shots were left. *If I know Max Duren at all, he got a very special pleasure out of interviewing a dead man.* The Nazi and his network of cops and judges, farmers and politicians. Casey was a dead man. Had been ever since he decided to connect with Clyde. The fix was in the minute he called him. Now Wolfe wants his story, and the FBI wants Duren. And once they get what they want, Casey's still a dead man.

So what does a dead man do, and where does he go? He remembered the long night ride from Mississippi to Phenix City, and the realization struck him that he never had a plan beyond putting a bullet between Clyde Point's eyes.

He continued northward toward Atlanta. Somewhere close to Senoia hunger pangs made him seek out a hamburger joint, where he ordered fries and a strawberry milk shake. He took it with him and ate it in the car in the parking lot. He was sipping the milk shake when he decided he needed a map. Rummaging through the glove compartment, he found a black rosary and an Esso map of the South. Just under it was a framed photograph of a young woman. He tossed the map on the passenger's seat and pulled out the picture.

The five-by-seven frame had a flap in the back so it could be put on a dresser or a desk. The woman looked to be in her early twenties with light brown hair, curls above her forehead and falling to her shoulders. She had a striking face, slightly slanted eyes, full of mystery, like a Gypsy, or a cat, prominent cheekbones, a full mouth. A locket hung from her neck, shaped like a rose. She was looking up, not at the photographer but at someone standing to the right of the photographer, and she was smiling. At the bottom of the photograph was someone's handwriting. *Kochanie, kocham Cie, Ewa.*

Wolfe had his ghosts, too.

Casey returned the picture to the glove compartment, hearing the writer's voice. *You're no murderer either. Orella Weicker told me that herself.*

*It's Orella, not your Gilda, who never betrayed you.*

The cops never knew he was in Myrtle Beach. *Neither she nor Gin told another soul.*

*She even had the stolen car charge against you dropped.*

And Clyde Point had nothing to do with it.

Orella.

*You got it all wrong, Casey.*

He drove, and he drove, until Atlanta was behind him and so was the daylight. He kept driving until he had no idea if he was in Georgia, South Carolina, or North Carolina. He drove, barely aware of anything other than the strip of road in front of him.

When he looked at the blond-haired stranger in the rearview mirror, he wondered who he was—Casey Eubanks, James Thompson, or just another dead man. He stomped the accelerator, and the Studebaker lunged forward. Just as it did, a car rushed up from behind and passed him like Fireball Roberts on a two-lane drag strip. He hadn't seen the car approaching. It was a '49 Ford, and from the front passenger window came a Pabst Blue Ribbon beer can hurtling back at him like a small rocket. It smashed against the Studebaker's bullet nose and bounced off into the darkness.

He leaned over the steering wheel and saw that a half-dozen yelling, laughing teenagers were jammed into the quickly disappearing Ford. He wanted to gun it after them, but a wailing from the rear made him ease off the gas.

His eyes shot to the mirror, which quickly filled with flashing blue lights bearing down on him at full speed. He pulled over to the side of the highway, one hand on the wheel, the other on the .32. The one thing he did know now was where he was going, and no blue light was going to stop him.

# CHAPTER 6

He rubbed his fingers across the cold steel in his coat pocket as the blue lights, the siren, and the revved-up 289 Power Pack/Powerglide flooded the space around him and then quickly disappeared into the night beyond. The cop was chasing the Ford and the teenagers, not the Studebaker and the two-time killer driving it. He listened as the siren melted into the night.

He slipped his hand out of his coat pocket and placed it alongside his other on the steering wheel. Then he leaned his head between them, a thumb to each temple. The air inside the car was hot and stale and still stunk of Martin Wolfe. The windows were down, but nothing stirred outside, just a thick steam bath that made it hard to breathe. He felt numb from no sleep, from being chased across the South by the hounds of hell. A kaleidoscope of images raced through his brain—Fay Spain playing with the straw in her milk shake, the face of Martin Wolfe's dead wife in the photograph, Orella in the rain. He pulled back onto the road.

When Casey was a boy, a revival preacher with a nose like a hawk once waved his forefinger at him and the rest of the back pew sitters resisting an altar call. This is what he said: "You ain't too young to go to hell!"

The preacher was right. Casey went. That's where he was now.

The preacher went on to say hell had no exits. Casey was going to find out.

He'd cursed Orella every single night since leaving Jonesboro, but now he was remembering the night he met her. Bux was newly married, on a thirty-day leave before getting shipped overseas, and he wanted to raise hell, so the two of them got three sheets in the wind and ended up at a barn dance in the country, where standing alone beside the beer barrel was a green-eyed, flaming redhead with a tiny waist and tight skirt that showed off her curves. She had round, cream-colored shoulders that were naked above a pleated, off-white blouse swollen with breasts too large for a small woman. He couldn't keep his mind or his hands off of her, and he got her to take him to the cheap frame house bordering the Vineyard, Jonesboro's whore-and-bootlegging district, where she still lived.

He left the next morning, of course, but he kept coming back, until she got tired of him leaving, married a preacher, got religion, and got pregnant. And after the preacher dumped her at the hospital door on delivery day, Casey was there to make her feel better.

Orella claimed she soured on preachers that day, but she still loved to listen to them on the radio. Something sure soured. The red hair went platinum, more orange than blond, the teeth went bad, and the curves just went. Booze, cigarettes, cotton mill life, bringing up a crippled, fatherless child, and Casey can do that to a woman.

His friends at the pool hall said things about her, bad things, and he'd either get mad or act like he didn't care. Deep down, though, he wondered, wondered whether she was a whore like his mother, like every other woman he'd ever known.

The night before he killed Bux Baggett, she got drunk with her neighbor Naomi and some fat guy named Paul. By the time Casey showed up at her house, stone sober, they were all full of cheap wine, and Orella was dancing the hoochie-coo to *Heartbreak Hotel* on her little box record player.

When he sat down on the couch, she danced in front of him, putting on a show for everyone, making a fool of herself, laughing, shaking her boobs and her fat bottom until he spread his legs and pointed to his crotch. She grinned, winked at Naomi and Paul, fell to her hands and knees, and crawled like a cat until she was between his legs. She put her head in his lap while he unzipped.

When he pulled it out, she stopped grinning and gave it and then him a green-eyed, love goddess, Rita Hayworth look that made him sick to his stomach but made him rock hard, too. She took him right there, in front of wide-eyed Naomi and red-faced Paul, took him all the way, and when he jerked her head up, his grip tight on that orange hair, she choked and coughed until he called her a whore and a cocksucker. She was so drunk she burst into laughter and then into tears, covering her mouth, and ran into her bedroom.

Yeah, his friends at the pool told him about the woman, and, sure, he wondered. But it was Orella who took him into her home when no one else would, never shut the door on him, fed him, nursed him when he was sick. For the first time in his life, he no longer cared if she was a whore. It no longer mattered.

He balled his fist and rammed it into Martin Wolfe's dusty dashboard. Blood bubbled up on his knuckles. Yes, Casey Eubanks was coming back to Orella again. One last time. It made no sense. Maybe, but what did? Despite all she would let him in.  She always took Casey in when things got too hot somewhere else, even had a key made for him. He still carried it in his pocket, and he was sure she hadn't changed the lock. He knew it. It was why he was coming back. That, and what the writer said, and maybe, too, the fact he had nowhere else to go.

Three or four miles up the road, he spotted the cop's Chevy Bel Air and the '49 Ford parked in the lot of what was once a vegetable stand. He slowed down as he passed. The cop and a raven-haired teenager with a ponytail leaned against the trunk of the Chevy while the others waited in the Ford. The teenager had her face just inches from the cop's and her hand played with the buckle of his belt. The cop watched the Studebaker pass, followed it with his eyes until it was gone.

By the time Casey crossed the state line into North Carolina, he was so tired all he wanted was to lay his head back and shut his eyes. He didn't trust stopping at a motel or roadhouse, but he slowed down when he saw a drive-in movie theater on the outskirts of Gastonia. The screen was visible from the highway, and a movie was underway.

A quick decision had him onto the dirt lane leading to the ticket booth, where he first caught the names on the billboard—Harry Belafonte, Robert Ryan, Shelley Winters, *Odds Against Tomorrow*. The movie didn't matter. What mattered was a dark place to park and catch a couple hours of sleep.

Maneuvering his way through the crowded lot, he found an empty spot near the rear, parked, and hooked the speaker up to his window like he had come to see the movie. Turning the volume as low as it would go, he slid down in the seat, and just before shutting his eyes spotted the couple in the car in front of him climb over the backrest and disappear.

A woman whispered "Earl" and made him look up briefly to see Robert Ryan straightening his tie while Shelley Winters watched from the bed. The next time he opened his eyes a bottle blonde with a familiar face was in Earl's apartment talking about leaving her baby alone upstairs. The baby was soon enough forgotten as the conversation turned to murder.

*"How did it feel when you killed that man?"* she *asked.*

*"I could've killed him all over, even though I didn't mean it,"* Earl *told her.*

*When he pulled the whore's gown open, her response was* *"Just this once."*

Casey's response was to fall asleep …

"Mister! Mister!"

Casey jumped forward into a strange place that he at first thought was along the banks of the Tallahatchie River. The stink of a cheap cigar and the sharp tugging at his arm brought him back to the drive-in. He pulled back against the unseen force and swung around to face a snow-topped man in a uniform, his withered face framed by the car window, and a smoked-down, still-burning stogie in the middle of it.

"Picture show's over, mister."

Casey shook loose the fog in his head and saw the big screen was blank. The Studebaker was the last car in the lot. The guard reached in, took the speaker, and hooked it back on its pole. He was so thin the flap of his belt was tucked in behind the walkie-talkie that hung at his side.

"Can't let you spend the night, though we got plenty folks think we some kind of pay-by-the-hour motel here."

Wheezing and chuckling at his little joke, the guard gave the Studebaker a good once-over, from trunk to hood, and his eyes sharpened as they drifted back to Casey's.

Dragging on his stogie one last time before stomping it in the ground, he walked to the rear, disappearing for a moment, and then returned to Casey's window, where he leaned against the car door and scanned the interior, a question spread across his face.

"Where you from, mister?"

Snorting loudly and clearing his throat, Casey rolled the window the rest of the way down and stuck his head out.

"Excuse me, would you?"

The guard stepped back, and Casey spit a mouthful of phlegm just to the right of the old man's feet.

"What the hell is it to you where I'm from?" he said, wiping his mouth. "I paid to come in here, and now I'm leaving, just like you want."

Casey turned the ignition and revved up the motor.

"Hold on. I asked you a question." The guard put his hands back on the door.

As the two sized each other up, a man's voice came out of the walkie-talkie.

"Locking up," the voice said.

Casey's eyes went from walkie-talkie to guard. "Nowhere, old-timer. I'm from nowhere. Good enough?"

"What you doing with Tennessee tags? Tennessee's somewhere."

Casey cursed under his breath. "Look, I'm half-asleep. I'm from up the road. I just bought this lemon, and it's got the old tags on it. Let me go home, friend, and get some real sleep."

111

The guard pulled the walkie-talkie to his upper chest and held it there while he scrutinized Casey's face. "Folks don't usually come to the drive-in by themselves. That's kind of a strange thing to do when you think about it, don't you agree? Why don't you turn off that motor for a bit and let me check something out?"

The moment the guard put the walkie-talkie to his ear, Casey grabbed the latch and shoved the car door into the man's mid-section, knocking him back so hard he tipped off balance and fell onto the ground.

Casey rammed the Studebaker into gear and spun off the little ridge where he'd parked and onto the lane in front of him. Swinging to the right, he sped down to the turn and veered left toward the exit. As he approached it, another guard rushed out of the ticket booth. This one was much younger and bigger, but Casey was through the exit before the guard could stop him, barreling down the little dirt drive and onto the highway, where he nearly struck a passing truck in the northbound lane.

His heart racing, he quickly had the truck in his rearview mirror. The Studebaker showed more spunk than he would have ever believed. He sped down the highway, searching for the first promising exit.

By now the cotton-haired guard had phoned in the make and license plate of Wolfe's car to the police and highway patrol, too. The way the old man had sized up the Studebaker, the writer must have called out the dogs from the first phone booth he found.

The first exit that appeared led into a gauntlet of burger joints, filling stations, and truck stops. Losing himself in the late night crowd might be his best hope, he figured. Eventually the road took him to downtown Gastonia, where a cop passed him with a flinty nod. He took the next right onto a narrow, tree-lined street and followed it until it dead-ended at a cotton mill as big and ugly as Central Prison in Raleigh, a giant, green-eyed monster lit up like a Christmas tree and bordered on either side by rows of little mill houses identical to the one he once called home. Surrounded by a 10-feet-tall chain link fence, the hulking, six-story mill loomed over everything around it.

Casey came to a stop and let the car idle. The Studebaker was one of the few cars on the street. The clamor from the looms inside filled the night air as second shift droned away. Strolling the yard between the mill and fence was a lone security guard, taking a smoke and, every now and then, a glance toward the Studebaker. On the porch of one of the nearby mill homes sat a few first-shifters talking among themselves, their cigarettes lit up like fireflies as they drank from bottles or jars in paper sacks and then passed them along from hand to hand.

Even if it was a dead end, it was as good a place as any to wait things out a little. They wouldn't expect him to hide in a dead end. Besides, he couldn't take his eyes off the mill. It was the biggest he'd ever seen. Silhouettes passed by its green-tinted windows, stick-like shadows, heads capped or scarfed, sometimes bowed, as miserable as the minions of hell feeding the devil's furnace. Better dead than a linthead. That's what he'd tell Orella while rubbing the calluses on her feet at nighttime, feeling the heat come off them into the palm of his hand. Yet everyone he knew back in Jonesboro was a linthead if they weren't farmers, cops, waitresses, gas monkeys, pool sharks, bootleggers, or preachers. Like that sad sack bunch listening to Ala Gadomska.

Not a lot of choices, whether it was Jonesboro or Spider Creek, Mississippi. A woman like Orella or his mother Julep could wait tables for tips during the week and string tobacco for seventy-five cents an hour on Saturdays in the summer, or she could work in the mill for a dollar an hour year-round. That's what most everybody did. Bux worked in the mill. Bux's brother Jack worked in the mill. Casey wasn't working in any damned mill. Orella brought it up sometimes. It's a steady job, it's security, she'd tell him, and he'd tell her to go to hell. Casey Eubanks was no clock puncher and never would be. Someday he'd get the cash to buy that pool hall he always wanted, but he wouldn't get it punching a clock.

While Casey brooded in the darkness, one of the first-shifters rose from his front porch perch, clutching his bottle in a sack, and walked slowly toward the Studebaker. Shortly before he got to the open window on the driver's side, he stopped, pressed a finger to his left nostril, and blew hard. After taking a moment to survey the results, he turned to Casey.

"Mister, can I offer you a little shooter?"

114

A hillbilly in overalls, he wiped his nose and pulled a quart Mason jar out of the sack. The white liquor left in it was just below the *Ball* inscription in the glass. He looked Casey up and down, then chuckled and unleashed a kerosene-like vapor.

"Look like you could use one. It's home-made."

Casey took the bottle from the outreached hand and drank deep. The liquor had no taste, but it shot to his brain nearly as fast as it burned to his belly.

"Thanks," he said, clearing his throat. "I owe you, I guess. What the hell is it?"

The hillbilly laughed. "They call it radiator whiskey," he said with a nod toward the porch, "but I just call it stump. Fella I know brought it back from Johnston County. Said he bought three milk jugs of it from Percy Flowers himself. 'Course he's been known to tell a tale or two. What you think of it?"

Casey pursed his lips and blew off his own vapor. "I never complain about free whiskey."

"Park this ol' Studebaker and come over. We got a little party going over here."

Casey took another drink, wiped his mouth, and shook his head. He sat for a minute or so and looked across the road at the silhouettes in the mill windows.

"Gotta go, I'm afraid," he said, and he would've stopped there but the stump was already making him talkative. "Going to see my woman. Hadn't seen her in a while, but her door'll be open if you know what I mean?"

Casey tried to hand the jar back, but the hillbilly shook his head.

"We got more'n we need back on that porch. Tell your woman Jimmy Shines and his stump whiskey gave her man a lift when he needed it."

As Jimmy Shines walked back to the other first-shifters, a bit more unsteady than he had seemed before, Casey revved up Martin Wolfe's Studebaker and thought about Orella Weicker waiting for him in her tiny house in Jonesboro. A sudden, intense desire for her flooded him, but with it came an unfamiliar fear that maybe this time her door wouldn't be open. After all, the world thinks he tried to kill her, even if she knew Casey Eubanks was no murderer. He looked down at the stump whiskey in his lap, and he laughed. But it wasn't a real laugh. He turned the Studebaker around, and then he paused to wave goodbye to Jimmy Shines, who had just reached the porch. Shines didn't see him. He was talking to his friends.

Casey crossed the Wiggins County line a little after three in the morning, by which time the stump had run out. He'd nursed the jar without a chaser up I-85, across highways 49 and 73, and along state road 24-27, from Charlotte to Biscoe. Between Biscoe and Carthage, only the kerosene smell coming off the mouth of the jar remained, enough to make him wish he had more. He'd finished off the writer's pint, too.

Casey was flying high despite an occasional prickling inside his belly. The Studebaker was running fine for a 10-

year-old car. Running fine enough for him to talk to it like it was a living thing.

"Damned if I wouldn't buy you if I hadn't stole you first."

It was great on gas. He'd put some in just a few hours back even though the needle had hardly moved before or after. The windows worked, and the radio had a good sound. Wolfe had left it on a station out of Chicago that now was playing songs about three o'clock in the morning, whiskey demons, and cheating women. The music had Casey moving his head back and forth. He was flying high and feeling good for the first time in a long time, and he hadn't seen a single blue light or police uniform the entire stretch from Charlotte to Carthage. God was smiling down on Casey Eubanks.

*First damn time*, he thought to himself as he rolled his shoulders to the blues coming out of a tenor sax.

He'd reach Jonesboro well before dawn, early enough to catch Orella still at home. It was Saturday morning, so she likely didn't have to go to work. The thought of the look on her face made him pull the jar up to his mouth, made him forget it was empty. He laughed out loud and shook his head, not at his forgetfulness but at the green-eyed shock that would welcome him from the other side of that screen door. She'd curse, threaten, ball her fists, and then open that door and those arms of hers wide and tell him to get inside before somebody spotted him. That's what she'd do all right. He knew it. No matter what she thought about that night, about what he had tried or wanted to do. He knew Orella Weicker, knew her better than she knew herself. The fear he'd felt earlier was gone. He'd killed it.

He grinned and then laughed out loud. Static came over the radio, and he turned the knob to get back to the station. Instead he found another, this one playing the song about the man with the red Cadillac and the black mustache. That song again. He had just heard it, only he couldn't remember where.

Once he got east of Carthage, he was in home territory, or at least what was once home territory. From Carthage to Cameron and then north to Jonesboro, he knew every hill and valley, every turn row, turn in the road, and dead-end. Even if it was another moonless, starless night, black as ink, he could smell the old smells, the sweet-sourness of tobacco, the dry, crisp odor of the first or second priming already curing in the barn. He'd handed, strung, primed, and hung plenty of it as a boy, done it all, although never for long.

Out in the field or back at the barn, he and Bux would bolt the first chance they got, even after their grandfather threatened to beat them with a tobacco stick and tie their feet to a sled. They'd steal off to a hidden spot and smoke rabbit tobacco. Casey kept bolting after he became a man, running away from Jonesboro and Wiggins County, yet always coming back. Like he was doing now.

Shadows within shadows of old farmhouses and barns, tobacco fields and pine forests, glimpsed off his headlights, swept past him. In nearly every house was or used to be a close cousin, distant relative, or someone who knew one. He wasn't sure anymore. In the old days, Casey kept the family custom of never coming through without making at least a stop or two. That was before the doors started closing and people stopped being at home, even when their trucks and cars were parked in the driveway.

Sometimes he'd catch them by surprise, and what he saw in their eyes was enough to make him move on. Nothing needed to be said. He'd heard the stories told about him--that he'd killed a pinhooker at the tobacco market in Winston-Salem, that he was a hired gun for the Mob, that he was Frank Wetzel's accomplice when he killed the patrolman Reece in Ellerbe. It was all ridiculous. He'd laugh about it over bootleg beer at Pokey's Pool Hall, enjoying the notoriety, until his Aunt Jessie stood behind her hooked screen door one day and told him to please go away, until his cousin Myrt Critchfield threatened to call the law if he didn't get off her property.

Myrt's farmhouse was only a mile or so away. She and her sons Watt and Blue were once a hard-drinking, hard-living clan that ran liquor stills and bootlegged as far as back as Casey could remember, even back before her husband Cole died a long and ugly death from cancer in the 1920s. Her first-born, Watt, had been like an older brother to Casey after he and Julep were forced to leave his grandfather's farm. Watt taught him how to shoot and hunt, and run whiskey. Casey shot his first pool game on an old table Watt found in a junkyard and put in one of the backrooms of the house.

When cancer killed Watt in 1952, however, Myrt took it hard, traded in the liquor business for religion, the Bible-thumping, mean-spirited kind that only the worst sinners get. Whiskey had made her rich, though, and she wasn't about to give any of it back.

Just as he reached the top of a hill, the car dipped without warning and the pressure went out of the gas pedal. Casey pumped hard but got no resistance at all. With a rumbling groan, the Studebaker crested the hill and began coasting downward toward the bridge at the bottom. Tossing the empty jar in the back seat, Casey reached over and pulled the choke, but the engine was dead. All he could do was let it roll and look for a spot to pull over.

One glance at the gas gauge told the story. The gauge registered more than half full, just as it had done two hours before. Only problem was he couldn't remember it ever being anything other than more than half full. *Great on gas*, he'd told himself between Biscoe and Carthage.

"Damn, sonuvabitchin' gauge doesn't work!" he barked to the dead Studebaker, slamming his fist against its dashboard. "You sonuvabitch Martin Wolfe!"

By the time Casey reached the bottom of the hill, he wasn't flying high anymore. He wasn't feeling good, and the prickling in his belly had become more like the stabbing from a tiny stiletto. Rolling to a level spot on the right shoulder with the bridge a few dozen yards ahead, he pressed down on the brakes with a mumbled curse. After the Studebaker came to a stop, he listened to the silence from under the hood, sitting there a long time, jaw set, teeth grinding out curse upon curse. God wasn't smiling down on Casey Eubanks. He was grinning.

The tomb-like darkness loomed before him now that he'd turned off the headlights and the tiny lights from the dashboard had gone black. Unable to see, he noticed for the first time how badly he stunk. He hadn't changed clothes since Memphis, hadn't shaved, hadn't showered. He flipped on the headlights again briefly to check the road. Myrt Critchfield's house was close by, just past the bridge and to the south. Although he hadn't been there in years, he could find it blindfolded, which is what he would have to do in the kind of night that surrounded him. She ran him off last time, but he had no other choice.

Myrt used to have a gas pump in her backyard. It was fed by a fuel line that ran to a hidden tank in the garage. Bootlegger's special. If it no longer worked, maybe they'd let him siphon some gas from whatever they were driving these days.

After searching the dash pocket and under the seat like a blind man, he finally found a flashlight among the jumper cables in the trunk. The batteries were dead. Stepping to the front of the Studebaker, he gave its bullet nose a sharp kick before entering the dark soup that lay ahead of him, soup so thick he was barely able to see the bridge. Negotiating his way to the railings, thankful the bridge had railings, he crossed it and stepped carefully toward the red clay road that led to the Critchfields, where they usually kept lights burning. In the old days, they lived like bats, up all night, sleeping all day, bootlegging branded whiskey, working the still in the woods behind their house. Watt ran the operation, although every decision first passed through Myrt. Blue, roughly Casey's age, was simple-headed but knew car engines better than a race track mechanic. He kept theirs in good condition as well as did most of the work around the still. And he did what his mama told him.

Finding the red clay road, Casey turned south but made the turn a second too soon and found himself tumbling down into a muddy ditch that still had a pool of water at the bottom from a recent rain. Cursing aloud into a night where not a hoot owl or even a cricket or frog could be heard, he sat there a minute or two, dazed by the fall and the last effects of the stump whiskey, but conscious, too, of the mire around his backside and ankles.

For all he knew, a copperhead was sliding toward him in the pitch black. He pulled himself up and tried to kick off the oozing chunks of earth clinging to his shoes and socks. His pants legs were wet, and he found mud in his coat pockets and in his hair, too. The only thing he could do was wipe himself off and climb back up the hill.

The house was actually set back at the end of a long dirt drive canopied by trees thick with honeysuckle vines and bramble bush, and surrounded by woods so dense that only rabbits and Critchfields could penetrate them.

Casey searched the sky in vain for a star or sliver of moon to light the way a little. Still, he was surprised how quickly he found the creosote pole that marked the turn onto the dirt drive. Coming on that drive was like entering the black mouth of some cave within a cave.

Casey just let his feet be his guide up the middle of the rutted path, surprised that the first lights from the Critchfield house hadn't already appeared. He walked and walked, fighting off a feeling of dread at confronting Myrt again, but saw no lights, nothing but more darkness until he wondered whether he might have turned at the wrong creosote pole. The Critchfields once had a floodlight in the yard, always yellow bug lights on the front porch. Having no other option but to keep walking, he continued until he bumped chest first into the gate to the wooden fence that surrounded the house.

Immediately the low, rumbling growl of a large dog pierced the dark, like a warning from another world. Casey stopped dead and reached for the .32, knowing the animal could see him a lot better than he could see it, which was not at all. The crunch of grass several yards away made him pull the gun.

When he heard the second growl, and the labored breath that followed it, a memory came back to him, and he recognized it as belonging to Smokey Joe, Myrt's ancient pit bull, apparently still alive, twenty years old at least by now, a nearly toothless graybeard that once roamed the house at will but which was later consigned to the yard when he could no longer control his kidneys and bowels.

"Smokey Joe, you sonuvabitch," Casey whispered. "You ain't too old to know me. Come here, you old fart."

Silence. Smokey Joe was thinking.

"Joe!" Casey ordered, louder this time.

A lamp came on inside the farmhouse, followed quickly by the bug lights stretching the length of the porch.

Once Casey's eyes adjusted, he could see Smokey Joe in a clump of grass and weeds near the steps. He was on his haunches, wincing through the matter caked around his vacant eyes. The dog was blind, his smeller gone, likely his memory, too. The porch was bare. No chairs, not even the ragged couch where Casey and Blue used to sit with their .22's and shoot birds.

Off to the left at the edge of the woods was a blue 1957 Chevy Casey had never seen before, the same make as Luke Doolin's in *Thunder Road*. Casey could hear shuffling inside the house. By the time he went through the gate and climbed the steps, the door opened with Blue Critchfield standing behind the screen, in a sleeveless undershirt and unzipped pants, scratching his head.

"Blue, it's me, Casey Eubanks."

"What in the world," Blue said, rubbing his eyes but making no effort to open the screen.

Then, appearing behind him, as if materializing out of nowhere, was Myrt, wearing a long white night gown, her hair falling down to her ankles. Rolled up in a bun during the day, Myrt's uncut hair was the promise to Cole that she had never broken. It was as white as her gown. She moved Blue to the side with a claw-like hand, adjusted her glasses, and glared through the mesh at Casey, her lips curling when her eyes lifted to his dyed blond hair.

Smokey Joe slowly made his way up the steps and to a spot by the wall next to the door, where he plopped noisily. Blue took a step back, still trying to stretch the sleep out, and ceded the floor to his mother, like he'd always done and always would, even though he was past forty.

"Long time no see, Myrt. Sorry to wake you but my car ran out of gas a mile or so from here. I figured y'all might help me."

A heaviness crept into Casey's shoulders as he stood before the screen door and unforgiving stare behind it. An urge came over him to turn and leave, but to where? Nothing lay behind him except a dead car and a lot of night. It was hard to look at Myrt so he let his eyes drift beyond her to the hundred-year-old hall tree that had been in the same spot since he was a boy. On the wall beside it were the Ten Commandments, in bold print and a fancy frame. This was new.

After making Casey wait long enough for Smokey Joe to start snoring, Myrt finally spoke, her voice just a shadow of what he remembered but with the same sanctimonious finality that it had the last time he heard it.

"You runnin' from the law, Casey. You killed your cousin Bux, and run off, on the day Our Lord was crucified, no less. No tellin' what you done since then, but now you come back, thinkin' I'd take you in like I did when you were a little boy and your mama was whoring around."

She produced a handkerchief that had been hidden in the palm of her hand, put it to her nose, and blew softly into it. Casey waited for the rest of it.

"You think the law won't look for you here? They know you, and they know what you up to, and they going to get you, too. Sooner or later, they going to get you."

As she spoke, the scent of rosewater drifted across the space between them. He searched for words but only found lies.

"I never killed Bux Baggett, Myrt. It was one of those pimps down in the Vineyard killed him. I knew they'd blame me and that's why I ran."

"Goddam lie," Blue blurted, and Myrt immediately slapped his face hard with the back of her hand.

"You don't curse in this house, you hear me?"

Blue rubbed his raw cheek without saying anything.

"I lost my Cole and then I lost Watt, and I saw I'd lose Blue, too, if I didn't give myself to Him"—her eyes lifted toward the sky when she said *Him*—"and so I did. Praise Jesus, we don't bootleg any more. We raise corn and hogs, and we live like the Lord wants us to live, me and Blue, and we don't truck with those who serve Satan."

She stepped closer to the screen.

"You come here lying about Bux Baggett, when everybody knows you killed him because of that slick-bellied Jezebel you were shacked up with, a woman with a sick child she won't even raise. You always had an anger in you. You had it as a little boy, and you got it as a grown man. I can see it in your eyes right now. It turned you into

126

a man who would lie, steal, sleep with whores, and even kill his own blood. Not that I don't understand some of it, being what you are, a bastard child who never knew his father, with a mother who took up with any man who'd have her, including niggers.

"Even when your grandfather had her fixed, like a bitch dog, to make sure she'd never breed again, she kept that itch between her legs, had it till the day she got the beating that killed her. Man did it might have been your own father. Course, it could have been any of a dozen men. Nobody'll ever know. All I got to do is look at that curly head of yours and that swarthy skin and wonder what bad seed brought you into this world.

"But I got to protect my son and myself. `Make no friendship with an angry man, lest thou learn his ways and get a snare to thy soul.' Proverbs Twenty-Two. What you need to do is turn yourself in to the law, and then turn your soul in to Christ. That's the only hope for you, Casey Eubanks."

She paused for a few seconds as if a revelation had come upon her. Casey searched her eyes, sensing a shift, but he couldn't read them.

"I look at you, Casey Eubanks, and I see Cain, a man who slew his own brother and then scorned the God who condemned him for it. Even now you have the gall to lie and deny what you did. What that tells me is it could be too late, that there ain't no hope, not for you, not any more."

127

Casey stood there in silence, tried, convicted, and sentenced.

"Blue, get a jug or two and fill 'em with gas. Take him back out to his car." Then to Casey: "'God knoweth the secrets of the heart.' You can't hide, Casey Eubanks. Not from Him. He knows every ugly secret in that lost soul of yours. Get on out of here, get yourself gone, and don't ever darken this doorway again. I'm going back to bed."

She turned and walked away, her steps hidden under her long gown, so light she seemed to float down the hallway. As Blue shut the door and went back to his room to dress, Casey stood alone with Smokey Joe on the porch under the yellow bug lights.

# CHAPTER 7

The early morning sky above the red-brick skyline of downtown Jonesboro was a brilliant blue. Casey drove north along the town's western edge, bypassing as much as possible to avoid cops and familiar faces on the way to Vineyard Road, which would take him to Orella's house on Vanity Street.

To get to Vineyard, he had to make his way around sprawling McDavie's Mills in the town's northwestern corner, going past its towering brick chimneys and the gated parking lot where he used to wait for Orella to finish her shift. A few cars were in the lot even though it was daybreak on a Saturday morning.

At the railing that stretched along the building's main entrance were several men making small talk, some holding Thermos bottles, all with burning cigarettes, getting a last smoke before their shift began. One of them, standing away from the others, an old man wearing a railroad cap with his company greens, followed the Studebaker as it passed by. Casey kept his eyes to the road. *Make no friendship with an angry man*, she'd said. *Cain*, she'd called him. *Lost soul.* She didn't say *nigger*, but he'd heard it loud and clear. It wasn't the first time.

Myrt Critchfield had always been a hard woman, strict and unrelenting with her boys and everyone else, all business, so tight with her money she'd squeeze the last penny out of every boozehound who weathered a freezing rain to buy her rot-your-gut whiskey. He thought of her standing there judging him, judging Orella, behind that screen door, her white gown, that long hair, those eyes moving from head to toe, full of condemnation, a woman saved and sanctified after thirty years of bootlegging.

Casey knew a verse or two from the Bible himself. *Woe unto you, you white sepulchers, full of dead men's bones and uncleanness.* His grandfather taught him that one after hearing a preacher he didn't like. Watt knew his shake-'em-down mother. *Daddy said she used to wipe her ass with a corncob.* He whispered when he told it, but they laughed so hard they cried.

The cool morning air coming through the open windows helped clear Casey's head as he tried to focus on what he was about to do. He drove slowly along the familiar streets, across the Southern Seaboard rail line, and north past gone-to-seed Victorian homes, two- and three-stories tall with wraparound porches. A Friday night drunk staggered along Robert E. Lee Avenue, lips moving, eyes fixed on some invisible companion as he cradled a bottle in a paper sack in the crook of his arm. His sockless big toe sticking out of a hole in his right shoe, he stopped his conversation to assess the Studebaker passing him.

Casey had seen that drunk somewhere before. He was as familiar as the smell of this Podunk town, the smell that seeps into your skin and lingers long after you've left the place, making you curse it when you're there and miss it when you're not.

At the end of Robert E. Lee was a three-way stop with a Pentecostal Holiness church on one side and a corner grocery on the other. Off to the right was Vineyard Road, along which the landscape changed from old Victorian to nondescript bungalows and empty lots of overgrown grass, the charred ruins of what used to be a shack or a garage, weeds everywhere, forests of them rising up behind the houses.

Vanity Road was the last exit before entering the Vineyard, a stretch of Jonesboro off limits to most white people and mostly left alone by the police, a valley where muscadines once grew, giving the place its name. Homebrew had long given way to cheap store-bought or bootlegged, however, good enough for the pimps and gamblers who ruled the Vineyard.

At the corner of Vineyard and Vanity was a store hardly bigger than a closet. A sign asked customers to say Pepsi, please. Midway down one-block Vanity was

131

Orella's house, a two-bedroom frame set back from the road on an incline. A car Casey didn't recognize was parked by the road in front, an old-model Ford station wagon, blue with paneled doors.

Cars lined both sides of the street, most of them long past their heyday. Among them, however, were one red hot rod, a joy ride that somebody couldn't afford, and a late-model Cadillac. Casey eased the Studebaker onto the street and down to within a house or two of Orella's, where he found an open spot to park. The Studebaker idled for a while but then finally went silent when Casey saw a light burning behind the curtain in her front room.

A shadow passed between the light and the curtain. Casey shifted in his seat, catching a glimpse of himself in the mirror. Red eyes stared back at him. His left cheek was still marked from the bruise Ala Gadomska gave him when she smashed a rock against it. He felt a sinking of his resolve, the cocksure arrogance that Orella would simply open her door and her arms to him. In its place was the same strange fear he had felt pulling away from Jimmy Shines and that cotton mill in Gastonia. He looked up and down the street. Maybe he was about to make the same mistake he made when he thought no one would suspect him of returning to Phenix City. Maybe cops were waiting behind that closed curtain in Orella's window.

He tracked the twisted trail of his stupidity over the last several days—the eyewitnesses who could identify him in a mile-long lineup, the double cross that had made him a patsy for Max Duren and Clyde Point, the police and mobsters chasing him from one end of the South to the other, and then back again, right back to Orella's bosom. No plan, once again, just a dead end and a crazy notion that made no sense.

A new resolve presented itself. He would leave Vanity Street, Vineyard Road, Jonesboro, leave Orella, leave it all for good and make the only smart move he had ever made in his life. He reached for the ignition, and the moment he did the front door of Orella's house opened. His fingers froze.

As she stepped out onto the little porch, every memory he ever had of her wanted to crowd his brain, the only woman he had ever wanted to come back to his entire life, a woman he hated only the day before. She was dressed in a sleeveless McDavie's print dress, black spots on a white background, with white slippers. She had lost weight. Her hair was shorter and back to her natural red, no longer platinum orange.

As if sensing the eyes devouring her, Orella hesitated a moment and then slipped back inside the house. The movement startled Casey. He leaned closer to the windshield as if to will her back again. Seconds later, she re-emerged, this time carrying in her arm an open box with the top flaps up. He couldn't see what was in the box.

She walked to the station wagon, stopping when she got to it to glance back as if she might have forgotten something else. Soon she was driving down Vanity, going in the opposite direction from where Casey had come, onto Bragg Boulevard, where she turned right. Casey followed.

She bumped a curb with a rear tire when she was too wide making the turn from Bragg onto Robert E. Lee. Traffic was picking up—a milk truck, a Coca-Cola delivery truck, a taxi, a twin-finned Ford convertible with fender skirts and a butch-waxed teenaged driver who also looked like he hadn't slept yet.

Once onto Robert E. Lee, she roughly followed the same route Casey had taken coming in, going around McDavie's mill and continuing onto Highway 1, traveling due south. He kept back as far as he could without losing her. If she met Martin Wolfe, she might recognize the Studebaker. He wondered where she was going and what was in that package. Wherever she was going, he'd soon be face to face with her. Gone were all those nights he consigned her to hell, vowing never to be fooled again. For the first time in a long time he noticed the old stirring in his groin that he always had when he came back to Orella. Despite everything, she made him feel like a man, not a chased animal or half-breed bastard.

She continued south down Highway One, passing through the little hamlet of Tramway, overcoming tractors hugging the side the road, steering clear of 18-wheelers making their runs to Atlanta or north to Richmond. A few miles past Tramway, she turned right onto 15-501. This was farming country, where the earth was white and sandy, the color of beach sand, soil that God made perfect for tobacco and pine trees. He knew this road as well as any road in Wiggins County, and as soon as she turned onto it he knew her destination.

He could already see it ahead, rising up from the horizon, the steeple of White Hill Presbyterian Church, behind which lay the last resting place of whole generations of Eubanks, Baggetts, and hundreds of other hardscrabble Scotch-Irish farmers, an old graveyard bordered by woods and tobacco fields. Casey hadn't been there in years, even though his mother was buried there and so was practically every other family member who wasn't still living. Even many of the living ones had their headstones there, already inscribed with only one date missing. Maybe Orella had family there, too.

Sure enough, she slowed as she reached the top of White Hill and made the left turn onto the dirt road that led up to the cemetery. The road continued in a half-circle around the church. As she came to a stop by the first rows of headstones, he entered from the other side of the road and let the Studebaker roll up to the church's southern wall, where he cut the motor. He had never once been inside the century-old building.

The Eubanks and Baggetts were Pentecostal, not Presbyterian, even though they were all made from the same stock. All except Casey perhaps. He slipped out of the car, leaving the door ajar to avoid the sound of the latch catching, and found a spot where he could watch her. She was walking along a row of what Casey knew to be Baggett graves. He could finally see what she carried with her—flowers in a vase that she must have had in the open box to keep them from tipping over in the car. She stopped at a grave with a temporary marker. Holding the vase in both hands, she began speaking to the grave, but Casey could hear nothing but the caw-caw of birds in the distance. When she finished, she knelt down and put the vase on the ground in front of her.

Casey stepped out into the open and walked toward her, along the same row of dead Baggetts. Her back was to him. She was whispering prayers. When he was less than a couple yards behind her, he stopped to read what was on the marker in front of her:

*Burch Eubanks `Bux' Baggett*
*1917 - 1960*

She had brought flowers to Bux's grave.

His eyes ran along the back of her, from her head to the flesh of her arms. She had the porcelain skin of a natural redhead. The flowers were Easter lilies.

The whispering stopped. She must have sensed a presence behind her. He had no idea what he was going to say or how he would say it. So he opened his mouth and said the only word he could, a word more breathed than spoken.

"Orella."

She didn't turn around.

"Orella," he said again, clearly this time.

She raised her head.

"You come to kill me, Casey?" she said, her voice soft, like it had been when he first met her. Life without Casey had been good for Orella.

"I never wanted to kill you."

136

Even as he spoke them, the words sagged with the burden of all that had happened, the impossibility of ever forgetting it.

Then she spoke again, her face still hidden. "I brought Easter lilies even though we're long past Easter."

He turned to the trumpet-like white blooms reaching out of the vase.

"I'm terrible with flowers. You remember, don't you? Can't grow a thing but weeds, but these just bloomed on their own, right by my front porch. I didn't even know I had them. I think Naomi might have planted 'em to make me feel better. It was like a miracle. They were so pretty I had to bring them."

Casey had no words to say, so he didn't.

"I come from time to time, early in the morning so as not to … Well, I don't want his family to see me here."

Casey stepped closer to her. He had found the words. "Orella, I come back to you, to tell you … to explain … "

Before he could finish, she turned around to face him, her green eyes betraying surprise at his blond hair. Those eyes made him lose the words he had found. The woman he'd left at that juke joint was no more, the burden of that night suddenly gone, for now, an old, bad dream whisked away in the breeze coming in off the fields around them. She was pretty, prettier even than that other night, the one at the barn dance. It was as if he were seeing her for the first time, in a new life. She smiled, and in that smile Casey saw a flicker of hope that maybe this time, this one time in his sorry life, he had gotten it right. Yet, hardly had it appeared before it faded as her eyes moved to something behind him, filling with fear as they did.

As desperately as Casey wanted to hold onto that smile, he understood the moment he saw it fade, and he cursed himself for letting his guard down, for allowing the source of the fear in her eyes to slip up on him. It had even gotten close enough to become a voice just behind his left ear.

"My, isn't this a touching reunion?"

The voice was instantly familiar even though Casey had only heard it once and then just briefly. What Orella saw was the pug face of Joe Arles, Clyde Point's goon in Phenix City.

"You a little far from home, ain't you, Joe?" Casey said, eyes locked on Orella's.

"Been waitin' here for you ever since you turned chicken shit in Mississippi. Want it in your back or you wanna see it coming?"

"Ain't much of a choice."

"Going to be one or the … "

Before Arles could complete his sentence Casey had swung around with his .32 in his hand and was pumping bullets into the gunman's face. Arles stumbled back, managing to get off one wild shot with what looked to be a .45 before crumpling to the ground. His face a bloodied waste, the goon fell into a sitting position, knees up and head back against the edge of a neighboring headstone. He might've been a man who had just sat down to rest a moment, but he was a man who'd never pose for another photograph.

Casey looked down at his bloody work, the work of someone with all the instincts now of a killer. Another dead body at his feet, another stranger, one whose own mother would no longer recognize. Casey reached down and pulled back the flap of the man's open-collared shirt. Inside was the golden medallion and its Aztec god, sprayed with blood just like the shirt and the headstone behind him. Casey read the inscription on the headstone.

*John Eubanks*
*May 1, 1869     November 26, 1943*

*Lydia Eubanks*
*March 15, 1879     March 11, 1944*

Casey's grandfather and grandmother. Something big and awful sprouted in the back of his mouth, and he coughed it out violently into the death that was all around him. He felt cold and sick, like some bad virus had crept inside him and was settling in.

Then, as if to lurch him back into the world of the still living, came the faintest of groans, lighter than a breeze, but enough to make him turn around toward the temporary marker behind him, where lay an overturned vase of lilies and Orella, slumped back to earth, her hands and arms outstretched on the ground, blood oozing out of a hole in her chest just above her heart. Joe Arles' wild shot.

"Orella!" he cried out as he went to her and knelt down to the ground beside her. Her eyes were closed, skin already clammy. She breathed in tiny fits and gasps, trembling slightly. Her hands clawed at the grass just beneath her fingertips.

"I gotta get you to a doctor!" Casey heard himself say as he pulled out a handkerchief to cover the wound. He hardly recognized his own voice. It seemed to come from someone other than himself. She opened her eyes. A glazed emptiness had gathered around the rim of them. She tried to speak but something in her throat made it difficult.

After much effort, she blurted out the word "Casey."

He leaned down close to her face, realizing as he did how much he had missed being close to her face. She struggled again to speak.

"C-c-c-all," she breathed.

"Orella!" he cried again. "What is it, Orella?"

With one last effort that took all she had left, she said, "In my purse … Call."

She passed out, and Casey immediately slipped one hand under her head and another under her legs, lifting her and himself up from the ground. Looking in every direction, as if for an answer to an impossible question, he turned to the station wagon. He ran to it, first to the rear but then to the passenger side and pulled open the front door.

On the seat was the empty cardboard box she had used to carry the flowers. Next to it was an open purse. He laid her down as gently as he could, knocking the box onto the floorboard and shoving the purse to the driver's side.

His lap would have to be her pillow. She groaned again, so faintly he barely heard it even though his face was just inches from hers. He ripped a strip off her dress and made a tourniquet out of it. After covering her with his coat, he rushed around the car to the driver's side and saw the key was in the ignition. He jumped in, grabbing the purse, and propped her head on his right leg. He fired the engine.

"Call! Call! Dammit, call who, Orella? Who?" he shouted, rummaging through the purse. Wedged between her lipstick and makeup kit was a business card.

*Martin Wolfe*
*Freelance Writer*
*Memphis, Tenn.*
*6-9653*

"What the …."

No time to figure it out. Only time to shove the card into his pocket and slap the station wagon into gear. He floored the gas pedal with his left foot still on the clutch. The wagon howled in protest. As he coordinated his feet, he made sure she was still breathing, then he took one last look at Joe Arles, leaning against Casey's grandparents' headstone, his nose, mouth, and chin ruins, his lifeless eyes fixed on the station wagon as if waiting for an invitation. Casey cursed Joe Arles and his corpse, and lurched down the sandy road around the backside of the church, past the Studebaker and past Arles' Cadillac, the same Cadillac that was parked near Orella's house on Vanity Street earlier that morning.

On the highway, he turned north and gunned it. The road was empty, so he pumped metal to the floorboard.

The old wagon was heavy and slow, and the needle on the speedometer trembled its way up to 40, 45, 48, 50, finally picking up at that point so that he was nearly at 60 at the bottom of the hill. No debate about where to go. The emergency room at Jonesboro Memorial Hospital was a joke, but he had no choice. The regulars down at Pokey's used to show off the zig-zag stitching they got for a busted head or a slit belly. The doctor-in-charge—Sylvester was his name—had come back from Korea a dope head, and it showed in his work. The joke was Orella's only chance to live.

When he got to the stop sign at the intersection with Highway One, he simply ran it and nearly careened into a carload of weekend vacationers probably on their way to Aberdeen Lake. They had water skis roped down on the top of their station wagon, the same make and model as Orella's. From the side window of the wagon two boys and a girl made faces at him.

Tramway was a blur. Casey's mind teemed with unconnected thoughts, fueled by a sinking in his gut at the silence beneath him. It was like some third presence in the car with them, watching and waiting. Even as his mind raced, he tried to hold on to the smile he'd glimpsed just before it faded, and he did until the Jonesboro exit loomed ahead.

"Baby!" she suddenly cried and tried to lift her head. "Baby!"

Her eyes opened briefly but then she fell back into a fitful silence. Was she calling him? Her kid? Maybe he'd never know. He looked down at the face that had haunted him day and night, and he cursed himself for all the things he'd never seen, never understood, for everything he had brought on her, including this.

He took the exit on screeching tires, sailing past the golf course and expensive doctors' homes that marked the divide between town and country. Soon he was at the turn for Hoover Boulevard, the Elks Club to his right, the city pool downhill to his left. Up the next hill was the Dairy Bar and over that hill Jonesboro Memorial Hospital. A quick check either way and he was flying down the boulevard, making the old wagon give everything it had.

"Orella! Orella! Goddamit, say something!"

Her breathing grew fainter. She was dying.

"Orella!"

A car pulled sleepily onto Hoover and narrowly missed getting sideswiped.

"Orella!" he cried out once more, but this time the answer was a police siren. In the rearview mirror was a black-and-white police cruiser barreling down Hoover at full speed. "Go to hell, you sonuvabitch!" he yelled.

Neither Casey nor the cruiser stopped at the red light at the top of the hill, and by the time he'd crested it the cruiser was on his tail, siren blaring, uniform and face a long shadow behind the steering wheel. A pickup truck pulled to the side to get out of the way.

"Then follow me to hell!"

The hospital was midway down the hill, and the entrance to the emergency room was at its rear, accessible through a half-circle drive. The wagon leaned hard as Casey made the turn, by which time a second cruiser had joined the caravan. All three wheeled onto the half-circle in a chorus of squealing tires and brakes. Before Casey could even open his door, the cops were out and on their feet with their guns pulled and fixed on him. Young cops, their uniforms crisp, their faces showing they had never dealt with anything like this before, one tall with a pale, angular face, the other a pug-nosed fire-plug.

"Hold it, mister! Hands up!" Fire-plug shouted, his hands shaking.

"Don't move!" the other added.

"There's a woman in the front!" Casey hollered back at them, his voice raw and trembling. "She's been shot! She needs a doctor!"

The cops looked unsure what to do next. The glass doors of the emergency room opened with a loud swishing sound, and two white-coated orderlies emerged with a gurney and looks of surprise on their faces as they realized they'd walked into a standoff. Standing there frozen, their eyes shifted back and forth between Casey and the officers, desperate for a signal. Behind them a small crowd was already gathering.

"Somebody do something! She's in the front with a bullet hole in her chest! What the hell is going on! Why aren't you doing something?"

The orderlies, built like linebackers, grabbed the gurney and rushed across the walkway to the station wagon.

144

"You!" Fire-plug barked at Casey. "Turn around, put your hands on top of the car, and spread!"

~ ~ ~

Wiggins County Sheriff Harmon Nix held the driver's license up to the desk lamp. Turning the laminated card from side to side, he narrowed his eyes as he angled his face in line with the light, the card with the lower lens of his bifocals.

"Hmmmm," he grunted, his mouth a curved line in a face of curved lines running from brow to jaw and cheek to chin. It was a long, sagging face with the look of an old shoe, brown and leathery with a big mottled nose in the middle of it sloping down toward his upper lip like the flap of a brogan. His reddish-brown hair, dyed and combed straight back, began at mid-scalp and fell longish behind ear lobes that hung down to his neck. He figured he knew the ways of the people in his county, including this one who had fooled those two young idiots in the Jonesboro Police Department into believing that he was someone other than Casey Eubanks. They were actually ready to take him at his worthless word.

Little brown eyes bore down on Casey. Nix was a cat whose paw had just landed nicely on the tail of a mouse, a mouse with rat pretensions.

He flipped the license down into the collection of pocket change on the desk in front of him and picked up Martin Wolfe's business card, which lay to the side of it. Tilting back in his chair and propping his knee against the desk, he scratched his face with a manicured hand. He wore a Texas-style black string tie on his short-sleeved, brown-and-yellow madras shirt. With his gray-green plaid pants, he looked like he and Speck Rhodes shopped at the same store.

"There's a powerful resemblance between you and a man named Casey Eubanks, Thompson," he purred, peering over the card. "Take that peroxide out of your hair, and you two could be identical twins. Why you even got the same tattoos on your arms. That's a helluva note, ain't it?"

Handcuffed, stripped down to his boxers, and split-lipped from the bully whipping he'd gotten after his transfer from the Jonesboro Police Department to the Wiggins County Sheriff's Office, Casey sat on the other side of the desk, breathing loudly through his nose and sucking down the blood from a loosened tooth. A yellow-haired deputy the size of a gorilla had slugged him twice with his blackjack when Casey resisted the strip search.

"I get a phone call. That's my right, and I need to make it."

Nix flashed a new set of dentures. "Son, you don't need a phone call. Salvation, that's what you need."

Casey looked away from him and surveyed his surroundings with its wood-paneled walls and forty years of citations, awards, photographs, and trophies, most of them related to fishing and bowling. A framed black-and-white photograph on the wall behind the desk showed Nix holding a mackerel that was as long as he was tall. Fellow fishermen looked on in awe. The caption read, "First Prize, White Lake, 1944." To the left of the photograph was a plaque.

*Wiggins County Sheriff Harmon Nix*
*Man of the Year 1958*
*First Baptist Church of Jonesboro*

"Martin Wolfe, huh," said the sheriff, reading the card. "Writer from Memphis. Hmmm. I know this fellow. He's been here before. He writin' your life story, Casey? Oh, I'm sorry. I mean Mr. Thompson?"

He flipped the card around from front to back. "Got an Atlanta number scribbled on the back here."

Casey stared tightlipped at the card in the sheriff's hand. He'd never even looked at the back of it.

"You know, last time we saw Casey Eubanks we had us a similar situation. Orella Weicker, a dead man, and a tattooed killer. Pretty amazing. What you doing with that little pea-shooter, Thompson, the one you used to, ah, defend Miss Weicker and yourself?"

Casey had told the story at the police station. A handful of one-sentence answers to a long line of repeated questions. He was Jim Thompson. He was a traveling salesman. He was trying to sell burial insurance to Orella Weicker. He went with her to White Hill so she could put flowers on a grave. A would-be robber came out of nowhere and started shooting. A traveling salesman has to carry a weapon these days to protect himself.

He didn't think they'd believe a word of it, but they surprised him. The officers were new, and Police Chief

147

Arnie Bean was away on business. When they learned the shooting took place in the county, they delivered him to Harmon Nix, who knew exactly who was sitting in the chair across from his desk but didn't want to lose an opportunity for a good game of cat-and-mouse. Nix had been sheriff of Wiggins County since the 1920s. He was the badge-wearing bootlegger working with Bux Baggett in the 1940s when Clyde Point tried to raid their liquor still. Nix was an old man, but he was still calling the shots in Wiggins County.

"A couple of the boys went out to White Hill. Quite a mess you left out there, Thompson. Got hyena blood in you? You know about hyenas? They go for the face. That's their calling card."

Casey decided he was tired of the sheriff's game.

"Have you checked the hospital about Orella Weicker? What do they say?"

"Doctor tells me the little slut's going to be fine. She'll be up and struttin' before you know it, telling me all about what happened at White Hill, and maybe now the truth about what happened out in the Vineyard this Easter. Why don't you save her the trouble?"

Casey lowered his head. She was alive.

Nix leaned across the desk. The cat was ready to devour its mouse. "Let's cut this bullshit, Casey Eubanks. Small town, big town, you so-called bad guys are all the same. You're a homesick bunch. Gotta come home one more time to suck on mama's tit even if it means putting your head in a noose. Just gotta come back. We been

148

waiting on you since Good Friday. Bux Baggett's widow and her four children been waitin' on you. So now you're back. You followed your nigger-loving girlfriend to the graveyard so you could wrap up your unfinished business, and this other sucker shows up."

Nix pulled a cheroot from his pocket and lit it. "Tell me about that sucker? What's his connection to you? This is Harmon Nix, remember? I know who you are. I knew your mama, probably knew your daddy. 'Course I'm like everybody else. I sure as hell can't be sure which one he was."

He paused to blow a stream of smoke in Casey's face. "Tell me about the sonuvabitch you killed out there at White Hill? Maybe he deserved it. Maybe you got a medal coming."

Orella was alive. Casey had nothing more to say.

Nix sent him to a seven-by-ten cell located at the end of a dark hall far from the other cells. It had a drop-down, chain-linked bunk on one wall, cater-cornered to a grime-covered toilet, and opposite a wall where a couple generations of Jonesboro drunks, thieves, and wife-beaters had left their poetry, prayers and curses against the horse-faced sheriff who put them here, against the cockroaches in their food, the stinking toilet, the beatings from Harmon Nix's deputies. One left a telephone number for any kindred spirit willing to meet him at the truck stop next Saturday night. Another simply told the world to go fuck itself.

The high-ceiling cell had no window or even a peephole. Only a dim light from a bulb overhead, and a slit in the door for the food tray. The floor and walls were marked with spots of dried blood. His bare feet stuck to the floor when he walked from wall to wall. The air was heavy with mildew and rot.

*The little slut's going to be fine. She'll be up and stuttin' before you know it, telling me all about what happened at White Hill, and maybe now the truth about what happened out in the Vineyard this Easter.*

She was going to make it. Casey didn't care what Nix thought she would tell him about White Hill or the Vineyard. She wouldn't tell him anything that hurt Casey. He knew that now. It had taken him a long time to realize it. Even if she did, it didn't matter. She was going to make it.

He stood at the steel door of the cell, leaned his head against it, and eyed the bunk. A thin sheet was bunched up against the wall. A striped pillow with feathers coming out of all four corners lay at the end. He stared at it until his eyes grew heavy and his shoulders slumped under the weight of a week of sleeplessness, long nights of running, of fitful dreams, sudden awakenings, hot, airless nights haunted by dead people everywhere he turned, nights spent in the driver's seat of automobiles and alone in strange hotels, in a limbo between reality and nightmare, and never knowing for sure which was which. A dull force began to move on him. He was tired beyond any tiredness he had ever known, and, as his body sagged under the weight of it, all he could think of was what Harmon Nix had said, that Orella was going to be fine. Orella was alive, and she was going to stay alive. Nothing else mattered.

He moved slowly toward the bunk, each step heavy, labored. When he got to it, he reached out like a child might to its crib and fell onto it, asleep by the time his head hit the pillow. The sheet lay undisturbed next to him. He was as still and quiet as a dead man, and he stayed that way until a hard, jolting smack across his face forced him back into the netherworld of the jail. Looming before his bloodshot eyes was the yellow-haired gorilla slapping his blackjack into the palm of his left hand.

"Sheriff tells me you being uncooperative."

Casey rubbed his jaw and tried to size up his chances with the stick-wielding six-five giant. Before he could, a second blow, this one from behind and directly to his right ear, knocked him off the bunk and onto the slick floor. He hadn't seen the second deputy although he could now smell his Bay Rum.

As he lifted himself, the gorilla dropkicked him in the gut and sent him hard against the steel edge of the bed. The second deputy raised his fist again, but this time Casey jumped to his feet and caught him with an uppercut that landed him on top of the toilet.

Casey turned to the gorilla just in time to catch a backhanded blackjack to the temple that blew out the lights. He dropped to the floor between the two deputies like a lump of clay. In the black formlessness around him, however, were powerful forces, and he could feel them striking against his face, his chest, his stomach, crushing blows that were dull and distant yet somehow deep and damaging at the same time.

# CHAPTER 8

Two deputies on the morning shift came to get Casey around nine. He was still on the floor of his cell, the exact spot where he'd fallen, naked, bloodied, bruised all about his head and torso, his right eye swollen shut. His boxers were gone, and his groin was black and swollen. He had thrown up during the night, a dark and bilious soup, and his first moment of consciousness was confronted by the stench of it. That and Bay Rum.

They pulled him up onto his feet, got him through the door, and walked him to a cubicle at the other end of the hall, one on each arm. Casey's clothes were in a paper bag by the entrance. Inside was an open shower stall. One of the deputies, a bandy-legged, hunch-backed pretzel of a man with a feminine voice, told him to wash himself off.

Casey nodded, shooting a one-eyed glance in the direction of Pretzel's partner but unable to get a fix on him. He smelled like the guy who sucker-punched him the night before, however. They watched him in the shower, and when he finished, Pretzel threw his clothes at him.

"Get dressed."

He did as he was told without saying a word. They watched as he slowly, painfully slipped on his underwear, his shirt and pants, pulled on his socks, tied his shoes.

"You got company," Pretzel said as he handcuffed the prisoner. "Walk behind me and in front of Waldo, and no monkey business."

They took him down another long hallway to a steel door with a double bolt. The latch was pulled, so with a hard shove Pretzel opened the door into a windowless room. Waldo left them at the door, and Pretzel walked Casey inside, where two men sat at a steel table. In one of the chairs was Martin Wolfe, in the same brown suit with the tie pulled loose.

In the other was a stranger, lean and fit, about fifty, graying, in a dark suit, white shirt, and thin, black tie. His arms rested on the table, and he played with the wedding band on his ring finger. The world-weary eyes and straight line of his mouth offered no reaction to the mass of contusions that sat down across the table from him and Wolfe.

Wolfe watched Pretzel step to the other side of the room.

"So you rednecks beat the shit out of him, huh." He turned to the stranger. "What do you say about that, Agent Beecher?"

The stranger nodded.

Wolfe gave Casey a sad, searching look. "I was sorry to hear about Orella."

"Nix said she was going to be fine."

Wolfe cursed under his breath. "She was dead by the time she got to the hospital. We flew up from Atlanta late last night. Hotel clerk told us about it checking us in."

Casey shut his one good eye and lowered his head. In a kind of echo chamber inside his brain, he heard himself yelling into the silence in the station wagon, Orella hearing nothing, eyes vacant, dying or already dead. He had wasted so much time hating her, and now he had run out of time. All he had left was that last smile, the one in the cemetery just before she saw Joe Arles.

That's what Casey had brought her, Joe Arles and fear. Arles had pulled the trigger, but Casey had killed her. *You come to kill me, Casey?* That's what she'd asked him as she knelt by Bux Baggett's grave. Orella had always been smarter than Casey. Even then, in the last moments of her life. She knew what his coming meant, even if he didn't know it himself. She knew what he had become. The trail of corpses behind him proved it.

"I killed her," he said, the words slipping out, thoughts turned into sounds, directed at no one but himself, yet Martin Wolfe and the stranger heard them.

"You didn't kill her," Wolfe responded. "Joe Arles did. We spent the night piecing that puzzle together. Ike Berliner sent him here to kill you, and just because you put a hole in Arles' face, don't think it's over. You're going to be a dead man, too, if you don't let us help you. Whether you're in jail or not, you'll be a dead man."

"Maybe he doesn't care," the stranger said without looking at either of them.

Wolfe leaned across the table and put his face inches from Casey's. Their eyes met. The stranger played with his wedding band.

"Make 'em pay, Casey," the writer told him. "They killed Orella, a woman who was trying to put her life back together. They want you dead, just like her. Make 'em pay for what they've done. You are only person in the world who can. Make 'em pay."

They sat in silence for a long while. The deputy grew impatient. "Better hurry it up. Sheriff's teaching Sunday school this morning."

"Go to hell, you pretzel-looking sonuvabitch," Wolfe told him.

"Deputy, let us talk with your prisoner," the stranger said. "I think it's best you leave us alone for a few minutes."

Pretzel wrestled with it but then stepped outside.

When the writer turned back to the table, Casey was staring at him. "How do I make 'em pay?"

Wolfe nodded toward the stranger. "With my help and the help of my friend here. Casey, this is Hardy

156

Beecher, an agent with the FBI. I've known him ever since the day his horse beat mine at the Montevideo racetrack in 1940. Beecher was what they called a legat for the bureau down there. I was chasing a story for a publication called *PM*. The city was crawling with Nazis. They'd even tried a takeover that summer. Alois Dürren was one of them, the man we now know as Max Duren, a Nazi in a business suit, running Indian slave camps along the upper reaches of the Uruguay and Paraná rivers. Good training for a future cotton mill industrialist.

Beecher and I found one of those camps, a rotten, snake-and-malaria infested hellhole where men, women, and children worked twenty hours a day building a logging road in the jungle, worked till they were down to rags on bones, wracked with scurvy and diseases that don't even have names. When they died, and that usually didn't take long, they disappeared, food for the crocodiles.

Duren and his *Kameraden*, people like Julius Dalldorf and Ernst Kapuze, were building a Nazi world, just like their counterparts back home, a world of slaves and slave camps.

"Eventually Duren was forced to slip out of the country, and we traced him back to New York, where he joined Fritz Duquesne, stealing documents that helped German U-boats sink American ships. We eventually lost track of him. I joined the Army, and J. Edgar soon had his agents chasing his real passion: commies, not Nazis. Still, we know Duren joined the *Werewolf* at the end of the war. This was an underground organization formed to infiltrate the country, build a network, keep the Nazi dream alive. I mentioned them before. They ...."

"How did Orella get your card?"

Wolfe forgave the interruption. "I told you I was up here. You were still in Myrtle Beach. I've been following this story a long time, following your late friend Clyde Point to Jonesboro, to Phenix City."

"My late friend?"

Wolfe pulled out a red handkerchief from his pocket and blew his nose. "They fished him up out of the Chattahoochie River last night. Got him one of those third eyes I told you about. Just above the bridge of his nose. Clyde made the mistake of convincing Ike Berliner to let him send you to Duren, and he paid the price for it."

Casey showed no reaction to the news about Clyde. His mind had already turned to the dead man's boss. "So Berliner was giving the orders. Clyde. Joe Arles."

"Berliner's trying to keep Duren off his back, and both are going to be profoundly unhappy when they hear how things turned out, that once again, you've escaped the jaws of death."

"Orella's last word to me was `call.' The Atlanta number on the back of your card?"

"I phoned her soon after you stole my car, told her I thought you were heading her way and to let me know when you showed up, me and nobody else."

Casey let that sink in. Wolfe knew he would come to her, just as he knew Casey would go straight from

Mississippi to Phenix City. Something about Casey Eubanks telegraphed his every move.

Pretzel returned and walked to his old spot across the room. He patted his belt.

Beecher turned to Wolfe with a nod toward the deputy, who glared at them and tapped his watch with a bony forefinger. "You need to get on with it," the agent said. "The natives are restless."

Wolfe looked across the room with contempt. "Hey, go tell the sheriff that my friend here still needs more time with this man. Soon as we're finished, we're coming to his office."

Pretzel mumbled something and left the room to deliver the message.

Wolfe to Casey: "Beecher and I have learned a lot about this case, too much to talk about here and now. I can tell you this, though. Orella Weicker loved you, and she tried to protect you. I think you know that and that's why you came back. She told you to call because she knew we're your only hope. Beecher and I met with the sheriff first thing this morning and laid out the basics of what we want to do. We're going to take you to him in a few minutes. All Beecher had to do was show the tin-pot dictator his FBI badge and talk about foreign enemies, and the old man thinks he's a soldier in the war against communism. He's putting you in the agent's custody. He doesn't know it but he didn't have a damn choice in the matter." Wolfe studied the bruises on Casey's face. "How bad did they hurt you?"

Casey shrugged, looked away. Orella Weicker had tried to protect him.

"Casey."

"Nix's part of it, isn't he? Duren and the rest?"

Wolfe shook his head. "We figure that's what Clyde was here to do, but he never got that far. He had a past in this town and because of it he screwed things up. Clyde played a dangerous game. He was a wheeler-dealer loose cannon who, when you get down to brass tacks, served no master but himself."

Casey thought back to Clyde's raid on the sheriff's liquor still after the war. The pattern fit. "So how'd he screw things up?"

Wolfe looked at Beecher, who blinked his approval for the question to be answered. "By killing Bux Baggett."

~ ~ ~

Nix had on his uniform, a crisp, creaseless, iron-pressed brown shirt with dark brown pants, and a holstered pistol over his black belt. He was at his desk, smoking a cheroot, reading from a file when Beecher, Wolfe, and Casey came into his office.

The sheriff looked up from the file and motioned for the men to sit. The cheroot dangled from the corner of his mouth as he assessed Casey's injured face.

"You must of run into a wall, son. Got to improve the lighting that end of the jail." A look of amusement spread across his face. "Fellas, y'all made me miss Sunday school this morning. Shame on you. I had to call in a substitute.

Ecclesiastes was today's lesson. 'Vanity of vanities, saith the preacher. All is vanity.'"

He rolled the cigar from one side of his mouth to the other.

"Eubanks, Mr. Beecher here says I should put you in his custody. Says you ready to make a turn and help the government with this case. What you have to say about that?"

Casey, numb from everything he'd learned in the last hour, heard the long-faced sheriff's voice but comprehended none of it. He could only comprehend his own unanswered questions. "Why'd you tell me Orella was going to live?"

Nix smiled.

"Sorry about that. Doctor Sylvester down at the emergency room gave me a wrong diagnosis. An honest mistake." He turned to Beecher. "I've talked to the district court judge about writing a habeas corpus in this matter, and he's willing to do what he can to help the FBI fight communism. He does what the hell I tell him to anyway. I'm troubled, however, Agent Beecher. This is a man who's killed at least two people, maybe more. I know Casey Eubanks. If this is what a goddam communist looks like, then Jesus, Mary, and Joseph ..."

Beecher finished his thought for him. "He'll be under my constant watch, sheriff. Eubanks is key to our efforts to infiltrate this organization."

Casey shifted in his seat. Only the handcuffs kept him from ramming Nix's cheroot down his throat. He caught

Wolfe looking sharply at him. The writer made a quick, short shake of his head. The sheriff saw it.

Taking out his cheroot and tapping the burned ashes into a tray, Nix jabbed the cigar in Wolfe's direction. "Have to say you got a curious choice of partners, Agent Beecher. Been wondering why he's part of this. Since when do reporters and the FBI work together?"

"He knows more about this organization than any man alive, including me."

Wolfe: "Never been one for rules, sheriff. I go where the story takes me."

Nix leaned back, contemplating that statement, and propped a black cowboy boot on the edge of his desk.

"Eubanks here widowed the granddaughter of an old friend of mine, left four children without a father. Baggett's mother died from a stroke after hearing about her son's death. Now we got this no name—no identification on him—out in the cemetery with a face that looks like a flat tire, and we got a dead, nigger-loving white woman with a bullet hole in her chest."

Wolfe had to weigh in here. "Eubanks didn't widow that woman, and that's why we wanted him here with us in this meeting. He needs to hear this. Bux Baggett died from a gunshot wound to the back of his head. That's why he fell forward, on his belly, and not on his back. The shot came from a .45, not from the .32 Eubanks had. We know that's what he had that night because Bux Baggett's own boy testified to it. Eubanks took Baggett's .32 out of the car, and he fired it into the air above the heads of Orella

162

Weicker and Bux Baggett, just like he meant to do. It's the same .32 he had on him when he was arrested yesterday."

*The boy.* Not since Casey's earliest nightmares about that night had he let himself think about the boy. Yet he'd been there in that car with them. Bux had dragged him along, and he had seen it all.

The sheriff dropped his foot down to the floor again and straightened in his chair. "So who fired the .45?"

"We know Clyde Point carried one, just like his friend, the corpse you found in the graveyard. Orella Weicker saw Clyde Point in the juke that night. She recognized him. He wanted to buy reefer, hell, buy the place. Clyde was trying to cut a deal when Bux walked in. Seeing Bux Baggett was like getting a chance to lance a festering boil."

Nix puffed thoughtfully on his cheroot.

"I know the history between those two. Might make sense. I remember Clyde Point, young upstart who thought he'd cut in on the local liquor business. It was Bux Baggett bit off Point's nose. Might be enough to want to kill a man. Jonesboro Police handled the Baggett shooting. Sounds like Arnie Bean's work."

Beecher straightened in his seat, motioned Wolfe to silence. "Sheriff Nix, your help could make the difference in the Bureau succeeding or failing. Let me explain. We appreciate you talking with the judge, but that's not all we need. In our first meeting we discussed the man who was killed in White Hill Cemetery, that he was an operative of this organization assigned to do away with Eubanks for a

163

breach of contract. We cannot let them know their man is dead, not for a while. No identification of the dead man exists, although we think we know who he is. As for Blondie," he said with a nod toward Casey, "his identification indicates he is James Thompson. That's even who the police believe him to be."

"I know who the hell he is."

"You're missing the point, sheriff. This fellow here and the man you found in the cemetery are actually very similar in physique. Who's to say the dead man isn't Casey Eubanks, or should I say James Thompson?"

The sheriff was listening.

"We need a week in which no information is released as to the identities of either man involved in this incident, not by you or the police."

Nix's brow slightly furrowed. "A week, huh?"

"That shouldn't be a problem for a sheriff who has run this county as long as you have."

Nix smiled. He took a long, self-satisfied last drag on his cheroot before he stubbed it in the ashtray and pulled another one. "Shouldn't be. The *Jonesboro Herald* don't print a damned thing I don't want it to." A thought struck him as he lit up again. "Hell, I might even have it leaked that we suspect the dead man to be Casey Eubanks. Then I hold a press conference next week and chastise the paper for publishing false and unsubstantiated rumors. I like to have a little fun with the newsboys."

~ ~ ~

Waldo appeared at Casey's cell door early Tuesday morning to take him to the maroon Studebaker waiting outside. For the first time, Casey got a good look at the Bay Rum deputy. He was Casey's height but slim and narrow-shouldered. He had the kind of face that got lost in a crowd—button mouth, brown dot eyes, no eyelashes, light-brown hair. He left the handcuffs on Casey as he walked him down the hall. Nothing was said.

The sun was shining, and Wolfe and Beecher waited by the car. "Here's your prisoner," Waldo said with a sharp jab of his billy stick to Casey's lower back.

As the deputy turned to walk away, Beecher stopped him. "Aren't you forgetting something?" He glanced down at Casey's handcuffed hands.

Waldo nodded, but the moment he unlocked the cuffs he got a hard right rammed into his belly, bending him double. As Wolfe and Beecher studied the sky, a second right went up the deputy's rib cage, shoving the air out of him. His knees crumpled, but Casey stopped him from falling by pinning him against the Studebaker. "Think about me next time you sucker punch a guy. Think about me outside this jail thinking about you."

~ ~ ~

They left in Wolfe's Studebaker, retracing the route Casey had taken to Jonesboro until they got to Cameron, where they continued going south on Highway 1, through Southern Pines and Rockingham, in the direction of Cheraw, South Carolina. For much of it they rode in silence, with Wolfe driving, Beecher in the front passenger's seat, and Casey in the back.

"You need to get that gas gauge fixed," Casey grumbled at one point.

Wolfe scratched the stubble on his chin. "Why? I like to leave little surprises for people who steal my car."

They watched the landscape pass by, leaving each to his own thoughts, Casey's taking him back to Orella, to Clyde, through the string of dead bodies he'd left behind like a day's catch at the pier, all for a murder he never committed, dark, bottomless thoughts interrupted only by Wolfe's occasional comments about this town or that town. The writer seemed to know somebody or somebody who knew somebody in every backwater hole-in-the-road in the South.

When they finally pulled into a truck stop near Cheraw for a late breakfast, he knew the waitress, a pretty brunette with a penchant for winking. Her name was Mary, and she called him "Scoop." Beecher and Casey were "honey." They were her only customers. All three ordered the special: two eggs, bacon, grits, and biscuits.

After getting a fresh top on his coffee, Wolfe began laying out the details of the plan. Ike Berliner would quickly hear about the double shooting in Jonesboro. His absolute faith in Joe Arles would tell him the dead man in White Hill cemetery was Casey Eubanks. As for the man who brought the woman to the hospital and was later questioned by the law: likely a Good Samaritan who came on the scene. Arles was lying low. Berliner would give

166

him a day or two to make contact. That would give them time to lure Berliner out of his lair and confront him with the truth of his failure once again to have Casey Eubanks killed, a failure that Max Duren would find intolerable.

"If Arles was so good, why didn't they send him to kill the labor organizer?" Casey asked.

"Clyde Point had a better plan. You."

"I wouldn't place a bet on your plan so far."

Wolfe snorted and brushed his forefinger back and forth across the tip of his nose. "Beecher made that bet for the three of us. His hunches are better than mine. I'm too sentimental. I bet a month's pay last year that Chicago would beat the Dodgers because I liked Ted Kluzewski. Big sleeveless Ted hits three homeruns, and the damned ChiSox still lose the thing. Beecher bet the Dodgers. You remember Kluzewski, Casey?"

Casey shrugged. Wolfe shook his head. "Shit, you're hopeless. I'll make up for it this year. The Pirates are taking it all the way. Bob Friend, Vern Law, Elroy Face on the mound. Then Burgess, Mazeroski, Groat, Clemente, Skinner in the field. Solid. What say you, Beecher?"

"Pirates. Get back to Ike Berliner and the plan," Beecher snapped.

Casey dropped another lump of sugar in his lukewarm coffee. "Before you do, I've got a question. What else do you know about that night?"

"What night?"

"The night Bux died."

167

"More than you. I know Bux came to see you at Orella's that day with the black eye his brother gave him. They'd been fighting, old grievances, and he was mad and thirsty. The two of you drank all the liquor in Orella's house before taking off to get even. Next time she sees you is in front of the juke."

"I wasn't getting even with anybody. I just went along for the ride."

Casey never really understood Bux. "The war's over," he'd tell him, but Bux was still fighting it. He and his brother Jack were always at each other's throat. Mostly it was Bux. Both had fought the Germans during the war, but Jack had married one at the end of it. She had relatives up north, and they helped Jack get established. Bux just went back to what he was doing before the war. The drinking started when Jack moved back to Jonesboro to take a job at the mill as a supervisor.

"We found Jack, and the rest of the family with him. This time it got bloody, and Jack got hurt. Bux grabbed the boy when we took off. Why, I don't know. The man was crazy. Out of his head. Drove through the Vineyard like a bat out of hell. Then we spotted the pink Ford." He paused as he remembered his rage at seeing that Ford. "What was she doing there, writer?"

"It was a helluva Good Friday, I'll tell you that. What you didn't know was that Orella's preacher husband showed up at her house earlier that week. She never told you. Five long years, and he was back in town giving an Easter revival. Wanted her to take a fistful of cash in exchange for a quiet divorce. Didn't even ask about the child. She gave him the boot, but after you fellows left that night she decided the preacher's flock ought to meet the preacher's wife—in a flaming red dress."

The preacher in Orella's life was something else Casey never really understood, and he didn't understand it now.

"She got to the campground but couldn't go through with it. What she wanted then was hard liquor, but you and Bux drank all of hers. So she went to the only place in town that would sell it that night, that late. Big mistake. She might never have gotten out of there if Bux hadn't walked in."

"And she saw Clyde."

"Like I said, it was a helluva Good Friday, what the Germans would call a Walpurgisnacht, when all the dark stars are aligned. You once introduced Clyde to her, and who could ever forget that face? He was there that night, all right, watching everything they were doing to her. I later found an old drunk down in the Vineyard who was there, too. He told me he saw the white man with the strange-looking nose slip out the door right after the other two white people left. I believe Clyde Point stepped into the shadows, saw you pointing your gun at Orella, and took advantage of an opportunity. Who's to say you couldn't have shot both of them? Like I told the sheriff, Clyde carried a .45, and Bux Baggett died from a .45."

*So he'd aimed high enough after all, hadn't killed his own blood. He'd run for nothing, run straight to the man*

169

*who did pull that trigger. Somehow it no longer mattered. The dead were still dead, and he was alone, standing among them.*

"When you later went to get Clyde to help you down in Phenix City, he figured he could put a wrapper on what happened in Jonesboro and have you help him advance in the company at the same time. It's rather ingenious when you think about it."

Beecher motioned to Mary to bring them fresh coffee. Wolfe lit a Lucky, and the agent reached into his coat and pulled out an unopened pack of filtered Marlboros. "Let's talk about the plan," he said, his voice a monotone.

Casey and Wolfe watched him carefully pull back the cover on the soft pack. He tilted it toward Casey, who waved it away. Then he shook out one for himself and lit it with a lighter that came from the same pocket as the cigarettes. "The secret to getting someone to do something for you against his will is to find his weakness."

Then to Wolfe: "Explain."

The writer obliged. "Ike Berliner's weakness is women. Every whore Ike hires gets a taste of the boss before she gets the job. That's her ticket. The fat man thrives on them, and he rewards their loyalties and their willingness to indulge his peculiarities. He has a few that would turn your stomach. Girls who play their cards right get to be his pets. He's had a long career, and we don't know all the details, but we know plenty. Women got him into trouble down in New Orleans. He was part of Huey Long's machine down there—Maestri, Shushan, Weiss,

170

Jimmy Noe, all that gang. He kept screwin' the French chamber maids, running his mouth, making the boys nervous. He's the weak sister in Duren's outfit, and Duren knows it, but so far he's needed him too much to get rid of him. Berliner's a good businessman. Very smart. Like I told you, he knows the textile business, grew up in it, and he, like Tate Kettle in Memphis, helped Duren get established. He prefers running whorehouses, however, where the pussy never runs out. He's the one survivor of Phenix City's glory days. That tells you how smart he is. But for him women are his gauge of success, and he's always on the lookout for a new recruit."

Mary came with steaming coffee and their food. She and Wolfe exchanged winks.

Casey let her walk away, then: "So where are you going with this?"

"Berliner is like Duren. He rarely leaves his fortress. We need him where we can get to him because we have a mission for him. He's not going to want to do it, but seeing you is going to convince him he has no choice. That's why you're enjoying this free breakfast with us."

Casey looked at the agent, who quietly finished his cigarette and picked up where Wolfe left off. "We've found a new recruit who we believe will be able to, as Wolfe says, lure Berliner out of his lair."

"Okay, so you've got a decoy. Who is it?"

Casey glanced at Wolfe, who frowned and shook his head in silence. The agent spoke again.

"You know her, Eubanks. She's a pretty blonde with a Polish accent and a really nasty right."

# CHAPTER 9

Wolfe drove them into Atlanta late that afternoon just as countless thousands of secretaries, sales clerks, and bank tellers were getting off work and jamming the streets in the rush to get home. The Studebaker weaved through the crowds, the buses, the honking taxis to Beecher's downtown apartment just off Peachtree, where they planned to switch to Beecher's Bureau car, a two-door '58 Chevy Caprice equipped with a mounted radio-head that would record off a transmitter. This was something they'd need later, Wolfe said without elaborating.

When they reached the car in a small lot in back of the eight-story apartment building, Beecher said he needed to pick up a couple fresh shirts, so Casey and Wolfe followed him uninvited through a side door and up the stairs to the sixth-floor apartment. The wooden stairway was dark and grim, with the overhead lights at each corridor either in bad need of new bulbs or out completely.

"Elevator's broken," Beecher explained as Wolfe stopped the procession at the fourth floor to catch his breath. The banister wobbled the entire way up, and the stairs creaked. Nowhere was there another human being or even a human sound coming from inside the rooms.

At the fifth floor, Wolfe stopped to grumble. "Beecher, you can do better than this dump."

Beecher shrugged. "I don't need much."

Casey was breathing hard himself by the time they reached the sixth floor. The agent led them down the hall to apartment number 611. Inside was a single-bedroom flat with a small living room and adjoining kitchen. The window shades were up but the building next door blocked the sun. The place was sparsely furnished, clean without a dirty dish in the sink or a stray sock or even ball of lint on the floor, only a stack of newspaper clippings on the coffee table next to an eight-by-ten framed picture of Beecher, a woman with reddish-brown hair and blue eyes, and a boy in his early teens who looked like his mother—same color hair, long chin line, thin lips, wan smile.

Beecher disappeared into the bedroom while Wolfe stepped over to the kitchen to take a look in the refrigerator. Casey went to the coffee table and looked through the clippings. They came from the *Atlanta Journal*, *Atlanta Constitution*, *New York Times*, other papers. He read some of the headlines: "Secret Agents

Capture Top Nazi;" "Nazi's Argentine Refuge Exposed;" "Eichmann's Trial Worries Israelis;" "Israel Won't Give Nazi to Argentina."

Then he picked up the picture. Beecher looked younger, by years. No gray around the temples, fewer lines around the eyes. Familiar dour expression on his face, however, the same one he had when he returned from the bedroom with a couple of white shirts on hangers.

"The family, huh."

The agent stopped and watched Casey scrutinize the picture. Wolfe pulled a Pabst out of the refrigerator.

"Was."

Setting the picture back down, Casey turned toward the kitchen and walked past Wolfe to check the refrigerator, where he found a block of hoop cheese, a loaf of bread, a bottle of milk, a lone piece of apple pie, and several more Pabsts. "What happened?" he asked, staring at the pie a few seconds before shutting the door again.

Beecher, holding his shirts, looked across the room at the photograph as if it might give him his answer. "They left."

Wolfe held his Pabst up to his eyes and turned the bottle from side to side. "Hard to keep a family when you're in the Bureau," he said, his voice intended to sound distracted. "Takes a rare woman who'll put up with it."

Beecher stepped closer to the coffee table and studied the face of the woman in the photograph. "She put up with it nearly fifteen years. This was taken on our fourteenth anniversary, year ago last month."

Casey's eyes went from Beecher to the photograph and back to Beecher again.

"That photograph just a year old?"

The agent nodded. Casey started to say something but let it drop.

~ ~ ~

As night fell on the road between Atlanta and Columbus, a gloom entered Beecher's Caprice, a fourth presence among the three men. The Caprice had a mounted radio-head, but no AM. Mr. Hoover's orders. Of course, the silence had begun on the six-floor descent out of Beecher's apartment building, each man again left to his own thoughts, each respecting the others' need for it, all three thinking about the same thing—the photograph, the missing woman in each man's life, the empty room at the end of the day, the missed chances that could have changed things.

They stared at the Georgia countryside. Somehow in the shared silence an unspoken alliance was forming, not only due to the mission ahead but also to the concentric circles around the missing piece in each man's life. Whether Beecher and Wolfe were aware of it, Casey couldn't know, but he was, and he suspected they were, too. He knew the agent felt an instinctive contempt for men like himself, men who lived outside the rules, yet the agent was such a man, and so was the writer.

Beecher had been with the Bureau more than twenty years, yet here he was living in a tenement, deserted by

176

wife and son, still chasing the Nazi he chased when he was full of dreams and ideals. And the writer? A man living out of his car with a photograph of his dead wife, chasing that same Nazi as if this were the greatest story he had never written. *Are these two any better off than me?* Casey asked himself. Then he answered his question with another: *Better off than a man who crossed a thousand miles only to bring an executioner to the one person who might have actually made his life mean something?*

It was nearly eight when they pulled into the outskirts of Columbus. They stopped at the Rebel Yell, a collection of cottages arranged in a semi-circle around the motel office. On the office roof was a raging neon Confederate, sword in hand, facing north with a curse on his bearded face. The place was located along a frontage road littered with one and two-story pawnshops, liquor stores, loan operations, car washes, and one-room bars. The Rebel Yell was sandwiched between a pawnshop that advertised "Guns, Ammo, Watches" and a pool hall with *Sam's Billiards Emporium* painted in fancy lettering on a sign above the door.

Casey's eyes went immediately to Sam's, a converted storefront with 10-feet-long window panels displaying what was once the showroom. Inside were people crowded around the tables, bottles of beer lined up along the window sills, clouds of tobacco smoke hanging in the air.

"Let's shoot a game or two after we get set up," Casey said, his face just inside the open window in the backseat.

"Yeah, and let's call Ike and see if he'd like to join us," Beecher snapped as he pulled up to the Rebel Yell office.

Casey couldn't remember the last time he'd shot a game. He missed the feel of the pool stick in his hand, the smack of the stick against the ball, then ball against ball. That was the sound coming out of Sam's, along with laughter, curses, and a jukebox playing Kitty Wells.

The office door was open. As Wolfe went in to get a room for them, Beecher leaned out his window to listen to the conversation. The clerk was a man in a Hawaiian shirt with a belly so large it spilled over onto the counter.

"Need something with twin beds, plus a cot," Wolfe told him. "There are three of us."

"Three fellas in one room, huh," the clerk said with a wink and a wet-lipped grin after glancing at the Caprice. "Cozy. Pay in advance. Eight dollars for the room, plus two for the cot."

Wolfe pulled the cash out of his pocket and exchanged it for the key. When he got to the car, he threw it into Beecher's lap. "Number 3, over there to your left. He'll have a boy bring a cot over. Y'all go on in. I'm going to walk up the street a bit and get a bottle of something. Be right back."

The first thing that met Beecher and Casey when they opened the door to Number 3 was heat and dead air that hadn't stirred in weeks. The beds were made, but a film of dust and an assortment of dead bugs lay on everything. Casey went straight to the window unit and turned the air conditioning on high. He was met by a noisy blast of hot air. The unit rattled so loudly that he had to turn it down to low to get it to stop.

Eventually the air began to cool.

"Shit," he groused.

Beecher walked to the bed nearest the bathroom and put his bag down next to it. Turning on the light from the bedside table, he sat down and loosened his tie. On the wall above the beds was a painting of a plantation scene, Massa's darkies picking vast fields of cotton with Tara on the distant horizon. Facing the beds between the window unit and the door was a small stand that held a 12-inch Zenith.

Casey was moving toward the other bed when Beecher stopped him.

"That's for Wolfe. You get the cot."

Casey shrugged and put his bag down next to a vinyl chair in the corner by the window unit.

They waited a long time for Wolfe—Beecher sitting on the bed, Casey in his corner chair after trying the Zenith and finding it didn't work. They stared into space, saying little, and listened to the whirring of the window unit and the muffled laughter and music coming from Sam's. Something about Beecher suggested a sour mood.

After a good thirty minutes, Wolfe came bounding through the door with two sacks in his arms. One held a fifth of Jack Daniel's Black. In the other were Cokes, cheeseburgers in greasy, mustard-stained wrapping, and bags of fries. The room immediately smelled like a roadside grill.

"Sorry about the delay. Thought I'd kill two birds with one stone. Figured you boys were as hungry and thirsty as me, and, like Beecher says, we don't need to be out and about town." He looked around the room and frowned. "Man said his boy Jughead would have that cot over here in a jiffy. I'll go raise a little hell soon as I pour us a shooter."

The cap on the Jack Daniel's had just come off when Jughead tapped at the door. Setting up the cot alongside the wall to the left, the skinny teenager declined Wolfe's offer of a drink but with a furtive glance at the cheeseburgers. Once the boy left, Wolfe distributed the food, and he and Beecher shifted to the foot of their beds. Casey stayed in the vinyl chair. Wolfe filled his plastic motel cup to the rim. A raised hand stopped him when Beecher's cup reached a little shy of the midway mark. He then tilted the bottle toward Casey, who shook his head and grabbed a Coke.

"We need some ice to water this down," the agent said wearily. "I'll get us some."

Wolfe shrugged and drank in silence as Beecher left with the ice bucket. After studying the contents of his cup between swallows like a scientist inspecting a test tube, he lifted his eyes to Casey and nodded toward the door.

"He's a good man. You can trust him. Right out of the FBI manual—Fidelity, Bravery, and Integrity, even if he is a rogue. That's what the Bureau calls its troublemakers. Chasin' Max Duren when J. Edgar doesn't give jack-shit about old Nazis. Commies. That's the only war the Man fights."

The air conditioning whirred on as the writer explained how the Bureau had gone to hell, how a place called Apalachin proved it, how an agent named Milton Ellerin told J. Edgar who was behind the bombings in Birmingham, and the Man's response was to go after Martin Luther King. Jim Eastland and the boys in the Federation couldn't have been happier. So Beecher was taking a big chance. Hoover had no idea about this operation, and he'd have the agent roasting on a spit if he found out.

"Yeah, get sideways of the SAC, and it's off to Butte," Beecher said as he came through the door with the bucket of ice, "or worse."

Wolfe grabbed a handful of cubes and dropped them into his cup. "That's really why I'm here, Eubanks. Insurance. This is a black bag job. If we screw it up, Beecher can call me in to threaten publicity."

Beecher fixed his drink and took a sip. Then he pulled off his coat for the first time since Casey met him at the jailhouse. A gun was holstered to his waist, and Casey recognized it. A *Hoover Heater*, Model 10, .38 Smith & Wesson with a four-inch barrel. Watt Critchfield used to own one.

"There won't be any screw-ups," the agent said. "Besides, once this is finished, it's over for me."

"What's a black bag job?" Casey asked, taking a bite of his cheeseburger.

Wolfe finished his cup. "It's a bug. But let me explain. Near downtown Columbus is an old Oriental palace called the Windsong. Berliner keeps a suite there. Not like Duren at the Peabody. Berliner spends most of his time upstairs at his roadhouse tending to business, but he treats himself to an evening at the Windsong from time to time, especially if there's a woman he wants to impress."

Casey finished his sandwich and tossed the wrapper in a trashcan by the bed. "Like your decoy. The Polack."

The whiskey dance in Wolfe's eyes came to a stop. "Let me remind you, that Polack is my niece, the one you kidnapped, punched in the face and ribs, and left unconscious alongside a river. In the night. In a rainstorm."

Casey conceded the point with a short nod.

The writer eased back, pulled off his coat and threw it across the bed. He was wearing red suspenders. He put his empty cup on the floor to roll up his sleeves. Then he picked it up again and refilled it.

"Lucky for you, and for us, the face heals quickly. She's so damn beautiful a little makeup will cover what's left of that bruise you gave her. And by the way you wouldn't call 'em Polacks if you'd ever been there. Most heartbreaking damned place I ever saw. I was there after the war, doing a piece for *Stars & Stripes*. You couldn't help but fall in love with it, with the idea of it, if nothing else."

"Black bag job, remember?" Beecher said with a wary eye at his partner.

Wolfe lit a Lucky. "The hotel is run by a couple refugees from Mao's China, fat cat friends of the Generalissimo, who got his buddy Albert Wedemeyer to bring them to Fort Benning. Mr. and Mrs. Wu came by way of Hong Kong, where we believe they may have connected with Duren. He was there for a time. We have gaps in our information, though. What we're sure of is that they arrived in the States with a ton of cash, and they love Ike Berliner like a lost son."

Wolfe warmed to his story, rambled on about Joe Stillwell and the tragedy of John Service and the Dixie Mission in China until a fuming Beecher exploded. "For the love of Mike, Wolfe, let's skip the history lesson! Do you think he cares? Damn if you don't drive the wits out of a man!"

The agent stood up to shake off his frustration and walked around the bed to the bathroom, where he threw some water on his face. As he dried himself off, he looked across the room at Casey with an expression that wasn't hard to read.

"We're mighty touchy tonight, aren't we, honey," Wolfe said with a wink and a grin to Casey. He got up to peek through the pulled blinds. "Yep, a full moon."

As the writer settled back in his spot and lifted his cup, Beecher went to his coat, pondered it a second or two, and finally grabbed something from the pocket before returning to the bed.

"You slow down on that stuff," he told Wolfe. "We have a big day tomorrow."

The agent leaned toward Casey, resting his elbows on his knees, and held in his palm a small box-like instrument, three inches by two inches, roughly the size of a cigarette case. He hesitated a moment and searched Casey's face to make one final check before proceeding.

"This is a transmitter—it's powered by a low wattage battery, a quarter to a half-watt amperage," he explained. "It will be attached to Ala Gadomska, taped to her undergarments, and everything transmitted through it will be picked up and recorded on the radio-head that's mounted in my car. The car can be two blocks away, and it'll transmit just fine so long as there's no concrete wall in between."

Casey took the instrument and inspected it before handing it back. He then held out his Coke cup to Wolfe and motioned for the whiskey. The writer accommodated him, and then he accommodated himself.

Beecher resumed. "We've studied Berliner's habits very closely, and we used that knowledge to put Gadomska in his path. As we knew he would and made sure he did, he recognized her as quality female, a world removed from the usual fare at the Dixie Inn, something worth an evening at the Windsong. That's where they'll be tomorrow night, and we'll be close by. When the moment's right …"

"Or before," the writer interjected.

"The three musketeers ride to the rescue," Casey said, finishing the sentence and the long shot of Jack Daniel's Wolfe had poured him.

"Knights in shining armor," corrected Beecher, exchanging a knowing look with Wolfe that was indecipherable to Casey.

~ ~ ~

Beecher left early the next morning, leaving Casey handcuffed to the cot and Wolfe snoring loudly. The handcuffs had been a point of insistence despite the writer's assurance that Casey was no longer an escape risk. Later that morning, however, when Wolfe went to buy a newspaper and enough groceries to keep them fed that day, he left the handcuffs on—just in case.

"Where's the FBI?" Casey asked when Wolfe returned and finally freed him from the cot.

"Meeting with Ala, double-checking equipment, logistics, making sure our bought-and-paid-for contact at the Windsong forgets to bolt the back door tonight. If he weren't the best, you can bet your bottom dollar my niece wouldn't be part of it."

"Why aren't you meeting with her?"

"He's scared I'd tell her to high tail it to Chicago. Eva and I never had children, so Ala's like a daughter. Wouldn't do any good to tell her anything, though. She's in this all the way, wants it more'n we do. Headstrong, hard as a nine-inch nail. You know that."

Since Beecher would be gone most of the day, the two of them had a lot of time to kill. Wolfe produced a deck of cards, and they played five-card stud, five-card draw, the seven-card versions, and blackjack. They played for pocket change. Casey didn't have any, so Wolfe staked him. They drank lots of cold, stale coffee, picked at their food, and Wolfe kept the cap on what little remained of the Jack Daniel's. Casey won nearly every hand as his opponent waxed on with a nervous energy about a front-page story in the newspaper on the Congo, the UN, how Lumumba was the best hope for democracy in Africa. Casey let him talk himself into a 10-game losing streak.

"You this good at pool?" the writer asked, scratching his forehead.

After raking in the pile of pennies, nickels, and dimes that three deuces against a pair of queens had won, Casey pointed to his eyes. "Better. I can see a fleck of dust on an eight ball ten feet away. Once played Nubby Morgan in Rutherford. Ever hear of him? Only two fingers on his left hand but one of the best sharks in the Carolinas."

"You beat him?"

"Hell no, but I gave him a run for his money the first game or two."

"What'd you play?"

"One pocket, toughest game there is. Got to put all your balls in one pocket. Let's go over to Sam's, and I'll show you how good I am."

Wolfe waved his forefinger. "None of that now. I have a niece about to enter the lion's den. Besides, Beecher'd have me drawn and quartered. There's a side of that man you haven't met yet. Things get rough tonight, you'll see what I mean. I watched him once pistol-whip a back-talking Nazi caudillo in a farmhouse on the Argentine-Uruguayan border. He had the sonuvabitch on his knees praying to Mother Mary for mercy."

Wolfe stared off in the distance, remembering. Then back to Casey: "I know one-pocket. We're about to play a round of it but not in a pool hall. All our bets are on one pocket, and one shot, too."

~ ~ ~

Beecher returned after dark, and at exactly nine-thirty the three of them left the Rebel Yell in the Caprice. He drove slowly through the city to the south end of Broadway, past a stretch of department stores, jewelry shops, and corner groceries until he came to the turnoff to the Windsong. It was just a block to the east on a street canopied by oaks and maples in a neighborhood of Greek Revival homes and gingerbread houses.

The three-story, pagoda-like Windsong with its iron-gated balconies and Oriental lanterns was a complete alien. Beecher parked alongside a lot behind the hotel, a spot that provided a perfect view of the windows to Berliner's second-floor suite. The lights were on. Through the largest window, with the help of Beecher's binoculars, they could see a statue of Buddha and a mirror next to it. In the mirror were reflections of silk tapestry and calligraphy.

The street was quiet, and just a few cars were in the lot. Nowhere was there a cop or a security guard. A jeepload of trolling soldiers from Fort Benning swept past them, their laughter and catcalls piercing the breezeless

187

night air for the next block or two. Inside the Caprice the only sound was Wolfe's labored breathing. They waited.

"Tell me again what she said," he asked Beecher.

"You know what she said." Beecher's eyes stayed fixed on the second-floor suite. "Everything is set. At ten-thirty she arrives wearing the green kimono he bought her at the hotel shop." He checked his watch. "It's nearly time. Stop worrying. She's completely prepared, and I've covered everything else." A few seconds passed. "I will tell you something she said. It was this: `Let me work my magic.'"

Lighting another cigarette with a deep-lunged cough, Wolfe grumbled to himself, took another drag, and rolled down his window to blow a Lucky Strike stream into the night. Casey leaned forward with a question. He noticed Wolfe had his wooden nickel between his thumb and index finger. "Tell me again why he won't know who she is?"

"No photos of her got in the papers," the agent answered. "Duren himself made sure of that. No real reason why Berliner should know what Ala Gadomska looks like. Besides, he thinks his guest tonight is German, Zarah from Breslau."

Wolfe looked up from his talisman and spoke in a low voice. "She speaks fluent Kraut."

"Zarah?"

"As in Zarah Leander," the writer said. "Another somebody you never heard of."

Casey's thoughts had already shifted to the man in the second-floor suite. It was Ike Berliner who hired Joe Arles,

188

the thug who killed Orella. Getting Berliner put him one big step closer to the Big Mahah who set it all in motion.

When he looked into the darkness around him, the silhouettes of Beecher and Wolfe against the dashboard lights, down sidewalks that disappeared into the night just beyond the street lamps, he knew escape would be easy if he wanted it, but Wolfe had been right. He had no interest in it. His interest was in the man in the second-floor suite.

A reckoning was needed. His thoughts grew darker than the blackness around him. Casey Eubanks had killed two men in the past week. Each had wanted to kill him, and each had failed. He didn't ask for it, but this was what he had become, a hunted animal and a killer. Orella was dead. He'd never given her a damned thing in life. Maybe he could make up for that in death.

"Eubanks," the agent said as if he'd picked up where Casey's thoughts were leading, "when we get to the second floor suite, you wait outside the door till I tell you to come in."

Casey nodded.

The agent checked his watch. Reaching for the car radio, he eyed Casey again. "You're a man with a grudge, but you swallow it. We've got a mission to complete. Do you understand?"

"The Big Mahah," Casey said, looking away.

"What?"

"The mission."

Beecher nodded and turned on both the radio and the recorder on the radio-head. Wolfe shifted to attention.

189

"Time to hear lover boy make his move," he muttered with a toss of his cigarette. Casey slipped to the edge of his seat and tilted his head into the space between the two men in the front. Soon voices came out of the radio. She was already in Berliner's suite.

The first voice was a man's, distant, cooing, high-pitched, speaking German. "Komm zu mir, meine kleine. Näher. Einsam ist der Ike."

The sound of ice slapping against ice could be heard. Berliner was shaking his cocktail. In the distance was music, a jazz tune with a female singer.

"Helen Merrill," Wolfe said under his breath. "Whaddayu know. A gangster with taste."

Then came another voice, much closer to the mike, close enough to hear her breathing. It was steady and calm. Beecher and Wolfe exchanged glances. "Speak English, honey. Ich will kein mehr Deutsch sprechen."

"What makes baby happy makes Ike happy."

"Good idea meeting here, just you and me. Wonderful. I feel like I'm in China."

"You got class, baby. Too much class to meet in Ike's old roadhouse."

Wolfe turned to Beecher. "Good enough, I'd say. Let's go."

Beecher held up his hand, shook his head sternly.

The voices continued. "So you're from Lodz. I went there once, did I tell you? With my parents. Maybe we passed each other on Piotrkowska, me, a little girl with a ribbon in her hair, you a big successful businessman.

190

Would you have stopped to look at me, Ike, like you're looking at me now?"

Wolfe growled restlessly. "What's she doing talking about Poland? Does she want to tip him off who she is?"

Beecher dropped his hand, shook his head. "She knows exactly what she's doing. She's better than I thought she was. We could use her in the Bureau."

"Lucky for her he's thinking through his cock right now, not his brain."

A girlish chuckle came across the radio. Berliner's. "You talk crazy. I was in New Orleans when you were a little girl in Red Lodz. Come over here like I told you."

"I bet you would've liked me when I was a little girl, Ike. I was cute with my little blond curls, big green eyes. That's what everybody told me. Would you have wanted me when I was a little girl, Ike?"

The three men in the Caprice listened, motionless and silent, as if bound by the same spell she was weaving for Berliner.

She moved closer to him. Now they could hear Ike's breathing in the radio. He was breathing through his nose and making little moist noises with his mouth at the same time. It took him a while to answer her, and when he did, his voice was trembling. "Sure, why not? I bet you were delicious. I bet some man got a taste of you back then. Huh, baby? Hmmm. I'll think about that while you're on your knees licking my schwanz. Come here, little girl."

They heard a slap on a naked leg, more heavy breathing, then Ala, her voice as clear as if she were speaking directly into a microphone. "You know what little girls dream about, don't you, Ike? A knight in shining armor. Are you going to be my knight in shining armor, Ike?"

Beecher didn't wait for an answer. "That's our signal. Let's go."

They moved quickly out of the car and across the lot, through the rear door of the Windsong, and into a ground-level storage room where they found a stairwell. Beecher, Hoover Heater in hand, led the way up the stairs, taking two steps at a time. Wolfe, just behind him, caught his coat pocket on the railing as he made the turn toward the second floor, ripping the seam loose, and then stumbling over his feet as he reached for the next step. By that time, Beecher was at the landing. He waited as the writer righted himself and climbed the last few steps. Casey then joined them.

"Our contact assured me Berliner usually comes by himself," Beecher told them, "and Ala didn't signal that she saw any bodyguards. Still, we need to be on the lookout anyway. According to the floor plan, the suite takes up one entire side. The entrance is on the right, midway down. Ala will make sure we don't have to knock. I go first, then Wolfe. Eubanks, you come in when I tell you to come in."

When they stepped through the door onto the second floor, they entered a claustrophobic world of jade green walls and crimson carpeting. A scroll hung at the far end of the narrow hallway, covering the entire wall. Below the calligraphy were Chinese warriors on armored horses, gathered for battle by an ancient tree that reached into the sky. A chandelier hung from the hallway's gold ceiling, lighting up the faces of the warriors. Beecher walked down to the door, his .38 rising to eye level, Wolfe and Casey close behind, and pushed it open.

The agent and the writer swept into the suite, past mirrored walls and into the great room, where, amid grinning Buddhas and exotic plants, was Ala Gadomska in her kimono. Just beyond her, on a deep-cushioned purple couch, sat Ike Berliner, mouth agape, legs stretched out, his overripe melon of a belly, sagging breasts, and shrunken cock exposed between the flaps of his silk robe. Casey stepped to the side of the door to avoid being seen.

"Good to see you fellas," Ala told Ike's new guests. "For a minute there, I thought I was going to have to lick the man's disgusting schwanz."

She and Wolfe embraced as Helen Merrill sang an old Billie Holiday tune, *Don't Explain,* from another corner of the room. Beecher had his Hoover Heater pointed at Berliner's nose. The gangster blanched, the delicious evening he'd planned suddenly an Alptraum. A tic formed at the corner of his left eye. His was a face within a face, chin within a chin, all white except for the cherry red of his cheeks. The place stunk of lilacs, jasmine, and cigars, and with the piped-in air conditioning was as much like a funeral parlor as a lovers' den.

Berliner's eyes moved from the gun to Beecher's face, then to Wolfe and finally to Ala. Shock turned to rage. "What the hell is this!" he barked. Closing the flaps of his robe, he moved to lift himself up.

Beecher stopped him.

"Remain seated, Mister Berliner."

Berliner ignored the order and tried to stand anyway, and Beecher leaned in and slapped him across the face with his free hand. Berliner's cheeks shook, and a red streak as long as a middle finger appeared where Beecher's hand had been.

"I told you to remain seated. Don't make me say it again."

Shoulders gathering in defiance, the gangster turned again to Ala. "You bitch! Du verdammte Hure! You set me up!"

"Schweigen!" Beecher ordered and slapped him again, this time hard enough to send him deep into the couch. Stepping between Berliner's legs and bending his right knee into the man's crotch, the agent shoved the gun between mouth and jowl. He smiled then reached back and backhanded him. When he raised his hand again, Berliner let loose a pitiful yelp. Casey slipped into the shadows of the hall to get a better view.

Beecher backed away, lowering his arm. Ala searched her uncle's face for a hint at what was coming. Wolfe offered none. Meanwhile, Berliner worked to collect himself. He traced his fingertips along the periphery of his face, tracking the injuries the stranger had inflicted. As he did, the trace of a smile crossed his lips.

Then they heard the reason.

"Carl!" the fat man yelled toward a pair of French doors on the other side of a four-panel screen depicting magnificent gardens in an imperial heaven. Out burst a hulking, flat-topped redhead dressed in black and wielding a three-foot Dao sword. Shoving Ala to the side, he went straight for Beecher, and as he did, the reporter floored him with the same roundhouse punch that took out the kid outside Sleepy's Motel five days earlier.

Having dropped the sword into one of the flowering plants, Carl scrambled to get back to it, but Beecher caught him midway and crisscrossed his arms in a chokehold around the giant's head, twisting violently once to the right and then once to the left. Carl made no sound as he dropped from his knees to his elbows to the floor, his head dangling down like a broken jack-in-the-box.

"You've killed him!" Berliner cried in disbelief. "You've killed Carl!"

"Always guard your flank," Beecher eulogized quietly as he stood over Carl's lifeless body.

The agent grabbed a nearby chair and pulled it up to within inches of Berliner, who gave his dead companion a grief-stricken sigh and shivered as if a gust of cold wind had just passed through him.

"Ike, you're shaking. Little pecker's all shriveled up. You're wondering what kind of hell you just fell into, aren't you?"

Reaching into his coat pocket, he pulled out his leather wallet with his FBI badge and held it up for Berliner to see, then, arms on the chair's backrest, continued. "Carl must have heard us, knew we were here, but waited for you to call him before rushing out to help. Interesting. Strict orders, I'm thinking. No gun. Just a fancy carving knife. What repulsive little game did you two have planned for our mutual friend Zarah?"

Berliner started to speak but thought better of it.

"Well, we have us some untidiness here, but you can fix it. That shouldn't be a problem. Just take care of Carl like you took care of Clyde Point"

Berliner could hold back no longer. "What is it you want?" He was on the verge of tears.

The agent shook his head. "Ike, with what we have on you, you could spend the rest of your days in the Atlanta pen. No more pretty blondes to lick your schwanz. In fact, you'll be the one on your knees. Knees and elbows."

The old defiance returned. "What you got on me? Nothing!"

Beecher turned around to Wolfe, who then stepped in Casey's direction and motioned for him to come in. Casey stepped slowly into the room, getting a good look at Ala for the first time since that night at the bridge. As their eyes met, he spotted a hint of purple on her cheek. On her neck was the silver locket he'd noticed in the car.

Berliner glanced at the stranger's face, saw nothing he recognized, watched him and the blonde exchange looks. He was confused.

"Ike, let me introduce someone who's been anxious to meet you," Beecher said. "He used to work for you,

196

although I don't think you've ever actually laid eyes on him."

This time Berliner studied the swarthy six-footer in the ill-fitting suit, with his dyed-blond hair and black eyes. He turned back to Beecher, the sag of defeat in his shoulders. The tic at the corner of his left eye grew worse.

"I know who he is. I figured as much when I didn't hear from … ."

The fat man bit his lip.

Casey stepped closer and squared himself into a spot just to the agent's right. He thought about that reckoning that was needed.

"Yeah, you sent that punk to kill me, but he's the one that got left in the cemetery. He did get off one shot, though, and it killed my woman. She got the bullet meant for me. Left a crippled boy with no mother and no father."

He stopped, remembering Nix's words about Bux, the family he left behind. Dead people. Everywhere he turned. He wanted to put his fist into the fat man's face, but he didn't. The mission.

Beecher leaned forward in his chair. "Contract killing, murder. Ike, we got a can of worms here. Once we open it there's no putting the lid back. Prostitution, illegal gambling. That's just icing on the cake. And let's not forget Clyde Point swimming with the catfish in the Chattahoochee. Ike, this just doesn't look good."

Berliner's face sank, a penitent confronting the enormity of his sins, one with rat-like eyes staring into the abyss of his impending doom. Beecher wasn't finished.

197

"However, I've been very impolite. I don't think you've been properly introduced to the young lady in our presence." The green-eyed blonde in the green kimono stared at the penitent with no expression on her broad, Polish face. "This, my fat friend, is actually not Zarah from Breslau but Ala Gadomska from Lodz, by way of Chicago, champion of the working stiff, voice of the toiling voiceless in the sweatshops of the Deep South, most recently at a little garment factory in Spider Creek, Mississippi, called Bengal Britches. You may have heard of her. Why just the other day she survived a cruel plot on her life by a bunch of Nazi-led thugs and thieves."

Any residue of defiance in Berliner had now completely evaporated. He was smart enough to know the meaning of everything he had just learned—his face and body showed it. Still, Beecher wasn't going to miss the opportunity to tell him anyway.

"Yes, Ike, she's the woman your buddy Max Duren wanted taken out. You and Clyde Point sent him Casey Eubanks to take care of that very important task. But you and Clyde failed. You sent Duren the wrong kind of man, the kind of man who'd balk at killing an innocent woman, this same woman you were ready to have your way with this evening. What's Max going to say? He's not going to like this, Ike."

Beecher shoved his chair forward, got so close to Ike that the others in the room could see neither of their faces.

"You know what worries me most?" the agent said in a voice just above a whisper, as if he were sharing a secret.

"I'm afraid he's going to take it out on you, that he's going to blame you for all these troubles coming his way. Clyde paid for his sins. Will you have to pay for yours, Ike? In what dreadful way?"

As the full implications of the agent's revelations sank in, Ike's breathing became labored, and he put his hand to his chest. He leaned back from Beecher to get air. They watched as his brain worked through the information until he finally broke down. He cried and cried until Beecher backed away to give him space to rub his chubby hands into his chubby cheeks and wipe away the tears that now flowed freely. His shoulders and breasts shook. The flaps of his robe fell open again, exposing the nakedness that now pointed to the depth of his sins.

Berliner's thoughts were an easy read. Why hadn't he known the bitch was the same blond Polack Max wanted dead? Why had he listened to that schwein Clyde Point and sent Max some small-time hustler to do a big-time job? Ike was a dead man, worse than a dead man, because Max Duren would make death come slowly, painfully. He would stretch it out until Ike begged for it.

Beecher resumed. "Yes, Ike, what's Duren going to say when he finds out that not only is Eubanks alive and well but willing and ready to tell the world his story. Our writer, Mr. Wolfe, has been taking lots of notes."

Berliner stopped his crying to closely assess Wolfe for the first time since he'd entered the room, and he remembered once telling the reporter to go to hell when he confronted him on a street corner and started asking questions.

"You were even dumb enough to make a date with Casey's target, Ike," the agent continued. "Just how much patience do you expect Duren to have with you?"

While Berliner ruminated, Wolfe pulled a Lucky Strike from his pocket and lit up.

"Give me one of those," Beecher told him, arching his head toward him without taking his eyes off the wreckage in front of him.

Wolfe handed him his lit smoke and took another for himself. In the quietness that entered the room, Casey felt Ala's eyes on him. He stepped back and turned, and they stared at one another for a long time in a room filled with lots of thinking. She spoke first, with an intimacy that was somehow removed from the world in which they stood.

"You couldn't kill me, but you put me in that car and took me with you. Have you figured out why yet?"

It was a question she'd asked before, one that wouldn't wait any longer to be answered. He shook his head. "I don't know why." He wanted to know the answer, too, and he probed her green eyes to see if he could find it there, eyes as green as Orella's.

He turned away and looked down at the man in the black robe and remembered another unanswered question.

"Fat man, I want you to tell me something. If the plan had worked and I had killed her, and the deputy had done his job, what motive were you going to pin on me?"

Berliner was too wrapped up in his own misery to hear. They all watched as the agent reached over and with his .38 gently lifted Berliner's chin.

"Answer the man, Ike," he said. "I'm curious myself. Say Duren's plan had gone the way it was supposed to, why would Eubanks have done it? Surely you were privy to that much of the deal."

A handkerchief appeared from the right pocket of Berliner's robe, and he blew his nose loudly. After studying the contents of the handkerchief longer than would seem necessary, he said to Beecher, "He's a nobody. It would've been easy." He stopped to yawn—the yawn of too much tension, wide enough to reveal blackened molars in dire need of a dentist—then he spoke again with his eyes closed.

"The Kluxers. The Klan. It's who you always blame. They're idiots, nothings, like he is. They love it if you blame them." He opened his eyes to Wolfe. "And you reporters, you love it, too. What did that movie say? 'Round up the usual suspects'?"

The agent smiled, took a deep drag on his Lucky, and blew a perfect smoke ring into Berliner's face.

"Very clever. Very clever, Ike. Is that who Duren's going to blame when they find your body? What the papers going to say? The Kluxers thought you were a Jew as well as a Polack?"

Berliner fell into a long, pouting silence. At the end of it, he raised his head to Beecher with sad-eyed acquiescence. "So what is it you want me to do?"

201

"As exalted as you may be in your world here, Ike, you're not what Eubanks calls the Big Mahah. The one-and-only Big Mahah is sitting in his penthouse in the Peabody in Memphis. That's who we want, and you're going to help us get him. We're going to give you a chance to redeem your sorry self in this world, at least a little. A good word from the FBI might make your lot a bit easier. Right now, you're a lost soul, Ike, and the devil is licking his lips at the thought of getting his chops on you."

"What is it you want me to do?" Ike repeated.

Wolfe took a seat on the couch next to the fat man. "Well, we'd love to hear you give us a breakdown of Duren's entire operation, but ... ."

Berliner waved his hands vigorously in front of the agent's face. "If you think I know all of this, Mr. FBI, then you don't know Alois Dürren! He is a fanatic! He tells people only what he wants them to know. Nothing more. He's a mystery, even to me. I know when he needs me, when I need him, that's it. You think I go to his board meetings? I'm a hireling, like all the rest. You got it all wrong, Mr. FBI."

The contours of Beecher's face hardened, so much so the fat man shrank deeper into his seat. "Du sagst kein einziges Wort mehr bis wir fertig sind, verstehst Du mich?" the agent growled. Berliner quickly nodded.

Beecher straightened, glancing at Wolfe then Ala and Casey. "My apologies. Simply told Ike here in his native tongue to keep his damned mouth shut until we're finished." Back to Berliner. "No more interruptions, Ike.

202

It's very impolite. As the writer tried to say, we'd like to know everything you know about Duren—from business dealings to hit jobs—but there's no time for that right now. What's more important is the immediate task before us, the production of a little play written by Mr. Wolfe and myself, one in which you have the leading role. We're calling it *The Long Overdue Downfall of Alois Dürren, alias Max Duren.* You're not only the star, you're also going to bring down the final curtain."

Berliner stared at him with disbelief.

"You are crazy! No one brings Max down. You have no idea. And you want me … ? You are crazy."

Casey had had enough of the pervert. Moving to within striking distance, he leaned down and shook his fist in front of the fat man's nose.

"Let me explain something in my native tongue. The only damn thing you got to worry about is doing exactly what he tells you to do. That is, unless you want me to shove those rotten teeth of yours down through your bunghole."

Letting Casey have his say, Beecher kept his eyes on Berliner as he spoke to Wolfe. "What do you think? Should we let Eubanks have some private time with our chubby friend? Maybe that'll help him realize how completely his life has changed these last few minutes, how it will never be the same again."

Wolfe snuggled close to Berliner's side. "Excellent idea."

Berliner leaned away from the reporter as if fearing contamination and held up his palms in defeat. Casey backed up a couple steps, fist still balled, however. Beecher returned to center stage in Berliner's line of vision.

"Friends, I think Ike is going to work with us. He's a sensible man after all. Ike, let me describe the plot of our little play. Duren's a good German, a man who thrives on fixed schedules and punctuality, which makes life easier for folks like us who want to keep tabs on him. We know he spends most of his time in his suite at the Peabody, but he does venture out. He likes his driver to take him down into the Mississippi Delta in his big, black New Yorker so he can check out his property down there. He goes on Saturdays, always stops at a restaurant called The Nest for a midday repast. At one p.m., to be exact. The restaurant is on Moon Lake, near the river. Wolfe and I have studied the place, the layout, all of it. He goes there, eats, then he rides around the Delta surveying his holdings like the Big Mahah that he is. He'll be there this coming Saturday, which gives us two full days to prepare."

Berliner was listening. They were all listening.

"You know the place, Ike. Great fried fish and hush puppies—bass, crappie, catfish, even trout, Max's favorite. Has them specially delivered from the Ozarks and points north and west. The place used to be a casino back in the '20s. Still has the old blackjack tables upstairs. Duren occasionally meets his business partners there." With a nod to Casey, he added, "Tate Kettle, a politician or two. You've been there yourself, Ike."

"Kettle is always there," Berliner noted glumly.

"Ike, we want you to call Duren tomorrow morning, set up a meeting with him at The Nest for this coming Saturday. As far as he knows, you've gotten rid of Casey. Clyde's out of the way …"

"The union got voted down at Bengal Britches," Ala interjected, "so Duren should be feeling good about life. Even if it was by just a dozen votes."

"Tell him you've got a business deal for him," the agent said. "Tell him you feel bad about what happened, the rally and all, and you want to make it up."

"What kind of business deal?" Ike moistened his lips as he considered the possibility that his skin might be salvageable. He rubbed his chin thoughtfully.

"You've been his financial adviser for a long time. You've got another prospect for him, a mill perhaps, a timber company, a sure money-maker …"

Berliner shook his head but then stopped with a furtive glance at Casey.

"May I say something?" he asked meekly. Beecher nodded approval. "I have a better idea." Casey edged toward the couch again, but Beecher waved him away.

"Speak," the agent said.

Berliner collected his thoughts, bowing his head as if in meditation, and when he lifted it again, his eyes had turned cold and calculating.

"If you want to know the truth, I will tell you the truth. I despise Max Duren. I hate him. You always hate the person who makes you afraid. I have helped him in so many ways, and yet what am I to him? A Lodz German, a Polack with a German name. That's all I ever was. Yes, I'm willing to help you, but what will you do for me?"

Beecher showed no expression as he turned to Wolfe then back to Berliner. Was this a ploy, or had they really tapped into some caustic reservoir of resentment?

"The Bureau protects its informants, even a sow's ear like you. It can get you a new life. You may even get to eat pussy again before you die. Depends on you."

Berliner talked slowly and clearly, considering each word.

"Max has spoken with me several times in the past couple of years about a secret desire. He wants a gambling operation. Not in Memphis, or even West Memphis, but near, in the Mississippi Delta. Maybe not so much like my roadhouse here. More gambling tables, whores but not so many. He has this vision, you see, his own casino in the Delta, near the river. He thinks it would work, that people would swim the Mississippi to get to it. The law is no problem. They're in his back pocket. I've told him the idea is brilliant, but it will take much effort and my hands are full here."

Beecher and Wolfe looked at each other.

Beecher: "So you tell him you've been doing some thinking, that maybe the time has come to talk seriously about that Delta casino. What better place to discuss this than at The Nest? In fact, maybe The Nest is what you have in mind."

Berliner nodded. "Max is part-owner. He and Kettle. It's their place."

Wolfe: "Hardy, this could work."

"He would go for this," Berliner added.

"I think it's time for some good ol' Mississippi catfish," Wolfe added.

"But what's the rest of it? I get him to meet me at The Nest. What happens then?"

Beecher stood up and tucked a loose portion of his shirt neatly back under his belt. He slipped his gun into the holster on his waist.

"You go in and you talk to him. You get him to talk. We want Duren in a real talkative mood. The more he says the better."

Berliner: "And you'll be listening?"

"I've got a tape out in the car I'd like to play for you. You'll recognize the voices. You'd be surprised how the walls have ears."

# CHAPTER 10

The '58 Caprice left Columbus Friday morning with Wolfe behind the wheel, Ala Gadomska sitting next to him on the passenger's side, and Casey in the back. The plan was to meet Beecher and Berliner at the Jackson, Mississippi, airport late that afternoon.

It was a four-hundred-mile, seven-hour trip. Beecher had booked a flight for him and Berliner after the fat man called Duren, assured him the situation with Casey Eubanks had been resolved, and made his pitch. Beecher told them about it. Duren bit, but Berliner thought he heard something in Duren's voice that worried him.

"Why now?" Duren had asked. "What made you want to do this now?"

"I went through this month's receipts. We're rich, Max. Let's get richer." Then he added: "Besides, I owe you, Max. You know, the rally and all. I want to make it up."

Berliner was certain he heard a rawness, an edge, in the old Nazi's voice that meant trouble. "You're nervous, you're scared, and you're hearing things," the agent told him. "You were Johnny Cool on the phone. Duren's flying high these days. He's got no reason to have an edge. He's got dollar bills in his eyes, and he's excited. That's all."

The meeting at The Nest was set for a little after one p.m. Saturday. After they reconnoitered at the airport, Beecher would rent a car that Berliner would drive, and they'd spend Friday night at a motel in Jackson. Berliner had told Duren he was going to Jackson instead of Memphis because he was meeting a man from Louisiana who could make him a good deal on slots and other machines they'd need for a casino operation.

On Saturday, they'd drive up Highway 49 through the Mississippi Delta, dropping Ala off somewhere close to Spider Creek before proceeding north to Moon Lake. She would arrange for Wlodek to pick her up. He had recovered from his wound, and they couldn't risk riding into the town with her. Wolfe insisted on this part of the plan, and Ala resisted. Although she wanted to get back, even if incognito, to the workers at Bengal Britches, she also wanted to be at Moon Lake when they brought the Big Mahah down. She tried to make her case, but Wolfe told her it was too risky for her and for the plan.

"If you are spotted with us, that would be all she wrote," he said.

South-central Alabama rolled by with plenty of hours to think about what the next day would bring. The trip offered few stretches of silence, however, as Wolfe and Ala had too much catching up to do. He kept the speedometer five-to-ten miles above the shifting limits along Highway 80, through Montgomery, the towns of Selma, Uniontown, and Demopolis, and eventually into Mississippi. He couldn't push it too much with a fugitive as a passenger and a car that belonged to an FBI agent.

After resigning herself to the fact that she wasn't going to be part of the action at Moon Lake, Ala confessed she was as worried as a Polish *babka* about the workers at Bengal Britches. In her last conversation with Wlodek, he told her the situation was tense. The election had been rigged, and the workers knew it. Talk of purges and more stretch-outs was everywhere.

Wolfe tried to calm her even though he was worried about her safety, told her he wished she were back in Chicago where things were less risky. She grinned, shook her head, told him he talked like a Polish *dziadek*. He frowned, grunted, grabbed her hand and kissed it.

Casey watched, listened.

At times Wolfe became quiet and distant.

"A penny for your thoughts," Ala would say, and he'd shrug.

Eventually he confessed he was retracing the long trail in the hunt for Max Duren—from Montevideo to New York to Memphis. He had lost the trail many times along the way, lost it for years as he turned to other things, but here he was again. Eva had been part of it, too, the weeks and sometimes months spent away from her, time lost forever chasing false leads and forgotten stories. He said he thought about Eva a lot, about Poland, the war, the ghosts that had haunted her, her ghosts, his ghosts.

"It was all a long time ago," Ala said to him softly.

"Was it?" he asked her.

"I try not to think too much about things like that. I only want to think about today. "

He studied his wife's niece, her baggy khakis, thin black sweater, green scarf. She laughed and told him to keep his eyes on the road.

"I remember you on Milwaukee Avenue back in '56," he said, "protesting the Russians in Poland, the martyrdom of the workers at the Zispo plant in Poznan, waving a hand-made sign and singing … . What was that song?"

"*Polska Walczaka*"

"Of course. `Poland is still fighting.'" He looked away, repeating the words. Poland is still fighting.

"I can see you now, working the crowd, getting your interviews" she told him. "The wonderful story you wrote for the paper."

"You're right, that was a good story. The *Daily News* ran it front page, top of the fold. I lit a candle for the Poles that night at St. Stanislaus."

Casey spied the familiar gap-toothed grin. "Still got that voodoo saint around your neck, writer?"

"Better say a little prayer to St. Joe yourself." The grin widened. "Might come in handy."

211

"Bunch of voodoo," Casey snapped back, and Ala grinned this time.

"Better be glad Sister Faustina's not here to hear you say that," Wolfe said.

"Who?"

"One of the nuns at St. Mary's orphanage in Memphis, where I grew up. Over by the Pinch District. She took me in when my mother decided she'd had enough of me. Gave me this when I turned fourteen. Told me, pray to Ol' St. Joe and I'll never die in a fire, drown, be poisoned, captured or shot on the field of battle. You better believe I held on to this chain when I was in the Battle of the Bulge. Didn't get shot or captured either."

Casey listened as he viewed the passing landscape. He wanted to hear more. "You grew up in an orphanage, and your mother was still alive?"

"Yep," Wolfe nodded. "The woman loved her Bushmills more than I do. The Irish affliction. Our house caught fire back in 1925. I was ten. She and I got out, but my father and baby sister never made it."

"Guess they needed your voodoo saint." Seeing Wolfe's deadpan: "Sounds like your mother and my mother would've gotten along. Tell me about your father."

"He came from a long line of German foundry workers. Worked like a mule, drank a bucket of beer every night before he went to sleep. For some reason, never made it out of the bed that morning."

"German, huh?"

"Yeah, my grandfather came from Bavaria. Served with Mother Jones' husband in the Iron Molders' Union way back when. But you wouldn't know about Mother Jones, would you?"

Ala jumped in. "'Pray for the dead, fight like hell for the living.'"

Wolfe looked back over his shoulder. "Would you?"

Casey shook his head. Wolfe chuckled. "Of course the hell not. Why did I ask?"

Casey listened as they continued talking the wide range of their lives, Wolfe the writer, Ala the organizer, Eva, the point where their lives converged, the silent, unseen presence. They talked long miles about her, how she picked out the songs for her funeral, left Wolfe a locket to give to Ala on her next birthday, and left her niece a set of early jazz 78's to give to Wolfe on his. She'd ordered it months before. Ala pulled down her scarf and exposed the locket shaped like a rose.

"I always wear it," she said. "Where do you keep those records?"

"Back at my apartment in Memphis," he said. "I pull 'em out every May 25$^{th}$ I'm home and play 'em all night—Jelly Roll, Benny Moten, Jimmie Lunceford."

She pursed her lips. "That's not why she gave them to you, and you know it, but if you're going to do it, play them on her birthday, not the anniversary of her death."

They talked about the smile on Eva's face even as disease ravished her body and confined her to what would become her deathbed. It was a smile that seemed to come from another world.

Casey listened.

"You know," Wolfe said to Ala, his eyes on the road, his voice soft and low, "she's been dead twice as long as I was married to her."

A flock of blackbirds arced low across an open field, past a row of scarecrows, bent southward, then lifted and soared toward a distant line of trees. Beyond the trees was a gathering of clouds. Ala watched the birds disappear into the shadows. "Remember her singing the *Salve, Regina*? I would hear it in the hallway."

"Ad te clamamus,'" Wolfe answered, "'exsules filii Hevae, ad te suspiramus, gementes et flentes, in hac lacrimarum valle.'"

"What are you saying?" Casey asked.

"It's a hymn from us poor, banished children of Eve, sending Mary our sighs."

"From this valley of tears," Ala added.

She turned to Casey, studied his face.

"What was Orella like?"

He looked away toward the trees, toward the faraway clouds and the showers they were dropping onto some unseen field. "She'd sing hymns, too. Dance the hoochie-coo at night and listen to the radio preachers in the morning. She was a lot of things. You askin' the wrong person."

"But you loved her."

214

Casey pondered that statement. "Yeah, I loved her," he said finally. The words seemed strange coming out of his mouth. He wasn't sure he had ever said them—to her or to himself. Saying them once made it easier to say them again. "I loved her, but I spent a lot of time hating her, too."

Ala turned back to the passing cotton and soybean fields. Casey turned to his thoughts. He had loved Orella, and she had loved him, but what did that mean? She was dead because of him. The writer still carried with him a framed photograph of his dead Eva so he could put it on the nightstand in his hotel room. Casey had no photograph of Orella. What he had was her last smile just before Joe Arles shot and killed her, and what did that smile mean? Perhaps it came from another world, too.

*You come to kill me, Casey?* That's what she asked him, but then she gave him that smile. Her last gift. It was all he had left. That, and the fact her last word to him was *Call*, was why he was in this car, part of this scheme to bring down the Big Mahah.

He caught Wolfe's eye in the rearview mirror, and it reminded him of something. "Writer, you needed me at that Chinese hotel, needed me to make sure Berliner knew he had no choice but to go along with your plan, make him see you had him dead-to-right. I understand that. Why do you need me now? Why am I along on this leg of the trip?"

Wolfe lit a cigarette. Several drags later, he spoke. "Beecher asked me the same question. I went to bat for

215

you. Told him we need you, need your muscle if nothing else. This is a barebones operation. You are one more soldier on our side. We've chased this man for twenty years, and this is the closest we've ever come. Not even Beecher really knows what's going to happen at Moon Lake."

~ ~ ~

They met Beecher and Berliner at the Jackson airport as planned, rented a '58 Olds for Berliner to drive, and let Wolfe lead them to a little hideaway called the Red Chief Inn. It was south of downtown near the city's Old Hickory Park, just far enough off the beaten track to keep them from attracting attention.

Wolfe knew the place, of course, sometimes met sources there. The bartender and sole permanent resident, a man who concocted a mean tequila gimlet, hadn't cleared a profit in two years, and never betrayed a confidence, would appreciate the business, the writer said.

At the airport, they could see that Berliner was nervous, restless, and that it had fouled Beecher's mood. During the flight, the two had conversations that told the agent Berliner's fear was even stronger than his hatred of Duren. The fat man had stayed up much of the night working out the details of a bogus business model. He had to make it believable, damned believable, so that Duren wouldn't smell a skunk.

Berliner was going through with this—he had no choice now—but Beecher was worried the man's nervousness might give him away when he stood face to

216

face with Duren. The task that evening at the Red Chief Inn was to fortify the old gangster for what lay ahead.

A last outpost along the city's flood-prone frontier, where poor white seediness and the last high ground gave way to black slums and tarpaper shacks on stilts and cement blocks, the Red Chief was a tired-looking, extended bungalow and motor court with a long-neglected show window next to the main veranda that served as a rustic museum of stuffed wildlife, the dust-and-lint-covered trophies of long-ago hunts—a bobcat, a fox, an owl, two jack rabbits, two coons, and the antlers from a giant buck.

At the entrance to the dining room and bar was the inn's life-size namesake, a cigar store relic Wolfe called Kaw-Liga. Everywhere was the smooth black-red finish of polished redwood—the walls, booths, tables, bar. It gave the place a permanent warmth. The warmth glowed especially in the evening when the yellow polka-dotted curtains were pulled shut and the lights came on under the red lampshades in the booths.

A wide ledge bordered the windows. Lining it were framed photographs of Geronimo and Sitting Bull as well as Pancho Villa, Emiliano Zapata, and various caballeros and bullfighters. Next was a row of boxers—John L. Sullivan, Mike Glover, Pat Valentino, and finally a twelve-by-fifteen of Rocky Graziano in a zoot suit. This one was signed. "To Rusty from Rocco."

Behind the bar was Rusty, watching a boxing match on television. With his tangled bush of rust-red hair,

217

untrimmed mustache, flattened nose, and big freckled arms bulging out of his short-sleeved shirt, he looked like the fighter he'd once been, a middleweight like Graziano who'd once fought New York champ Billy Soose. Lost that one but won most the others. He wore a stained white apron and a permanent scowl. He hardly ever spoke, but when he did the voice was upper range Irish tenor. "Aging pug," Wolfe described it. Mostly he grunted and groaned, particularly now, shifting his shoulders and flexing his jaw with each solid punch on the screen.

Four of the five sat at the rear corner table with their tequila gimlets. Ala was in the telephone booth behind the bar making a phone call to Wlodek. The other tables were empty.

"I never drank a gimlet with tequila," Berliner said, drinking deep, forgetting his worries for a moment. Wolfe had earlier whispered in Rusty's cauliflowered ear, "Strong, very strong," and the boxer delivered.

"Rusty spent his last years as a pro in Mexico, way down in Jalisco, agave country. That's where he learned to make this drink. Picked up a special brand down there he won't disclose. I can taste it, but I'm too gringo to be able to identify it."

Beecher picked up his glass. "Bull's piss. I'd know it anywhere."

Wolfe took another swallow and nodded appreciatively at Berliner and Casey. "See? The man does have a sense of humor. But you know, I think he may be right. I would've never thought of that. Rusty'll be fightin' mad.

We better not tell him we're on to his secret. Look at him. He's not the kind of guy you want to upset."

They turned and assessed the sledgehammer hands. The ring commentators on the television were a distant rumble amid muffled yells and finally the sound of the bell. On the counter to Rusty's left was a small pitcher of milk and a nearly empty glass. Wolfe saw them make a mental note of it.

"Rusty's got an ulcer," he explained. "Too much El Viejito, too many mezcal worms."

Wolfe managed to get a nervous chuckle out of Berliner, but the mood soon darkened again. The specter looming over them, Max Duren, the henchmen he'd bring with him to the Nest cast too long a shadow. Casey felt it, too, and figured he may as well look it in the eye.

"Hey, FBI man, how about going over this again? The plan."

Beecher rubbed his fingers slowly along some carved initials customers had left in the table's finish.

"I'm putting the same three-by-two transmitter on Ike that I put on Ala. It'll work just like it worked for her. Duren will never know a thing. We'll be close by, less than a quarter-mile, recording every word that's said, close enough to come to the rescue in the great unlikelihood something goes wrong."

Berliner gazed into his tequila gimlet like a man contemplating his execution. "I was in the room one day when Duren took his revenge on some poor sucker who had crossed him," he said, his mind trailing back to the

219

event. "It was at one of Duren's graineries. They had the man tied up, his mouth jammed with cotton to block his screams, and let an auger chew his leg off. Then they let him bleed to death."

He spoke like a dead man, as if his fate had already been decided, and this was it.

"What had the guy done?" Casey asked him.

Berliner looked up from the memory and gazed blankly across the booth. The tic returned to the corner of his left eye. "It had nothing to do with what he did. It was what Max said he did. Max said the man betrayed him, the unforgivable sin, the one that deserves the worst punishment. Did he betray him? Even Max didn't know for sure. It didn't matter."

Emerging from the phone booth, Ala stepped over to the bar and asked Rusty for a double vodka. With a short nod, one eye still on the fight, he scooped ice in a glass and poured it full of Smirnoff. She walked it to the table with a face full of trouble. Wearing the same khakis and sweater from the day before but with a yellow scarf and black beret, she had been on the phone nearly twenty minutes.

"We got a problem," she said, taking her seat. The green eyes shifted from man to man at the table. "Give me one of those Lucky Strikes," she told Wolfe. He pulled one out and struck a match. She swallowed the first deep drag.

"The workers at Bengal Britches are going on strike."

The air around the table became as heavy as the redwood furnishings. The men stared at her as if trying to comprehend what she'd just said. Not the fat man, however. He understood. It was all over his face, particularly in the little chocolate eyes.

"What do you mean?" he demanded, barely controlling the emotion in his voice.

She sucked at her Lucky Strike and looked at Wolfe. "Wlodek said management put 'em right back on the stretch-out after the election. Double production, twelve-hour days, every day. No overtime pay. No extra break either, not till the order's filled. Those who can't do it are fired. They already fired several of the women who pushed hardest for the union. Wlodek says everyone knows the election was bogus. They did their own head count. The picket line'll be up when the factory horn blows at seven in the morning."

Berliner pounded the table in front of her.

"They can't do that! Max will be insane with anger, and he'll blame it on me." He rose inches from his seat, fear rippling through his body. "The plan is off! We can do nothing now! I refuse to commit suicide, do you hear me? He'll kill us all!"

The agent waved his hand in front of Berliner's face, and the old gangster retreated to brood.

"Ike, calm down. Think about this. You've already arranged to meet Duren at The Nest. He's going to be there. You think you can just not show up? Stop acting as if you still have a choice. You don't." The agent turned to Ala. "You've got to go to Spider Creek immediately and stop this thing, at least get them to wait one more day or until Monday. You're the only one who can do it."

Ala slugged back the rest of her vodka and wiped her mouth. She looked around the table at the four very different men waiting for her response.

"I've already called Claude Ramsay with the state AFL. He's sending a man over to take me."

Beecher put his hand on her forearm and pressed. "You brought him in?"

She removed the hand. "The only thing Claude knows is the situation at Bengal Britches, and he agrees a wildcat strike right now would be disastrous, that we got to have the union backing us. That's why he's helping."

Beecher turned to Wolfe, who offered a reassuring wink. "Ramsay's a warrior," the writer said. "Got to be in this damned state. He's all right. You can trust him."

It was all too much for Berliner, who waved at Rusty to bring him another drink. The ferret-like eyes bore down on Ala. "You must stop this." After realizing Rusty hadn't seen him: "Bartender! Another!"

The iron-jawed face slowly turned toward the table at the other end of the room.

"Just a fuckin' minute, señor."

"Check in with us as soon as you get there," Beecher said, tapping Ala's wrist. "Let us know the situation."

She nodded. "Claude's man will be here in less than an hour."

Beecher grabbed Berliner under the arm and stood up.

"Forget the drink. Let's go. Time to turn in." Then to Ala: "Tell 'em they can strike on Sunday if they want. Just not tomorrow morning."

She nodded grimly as the two walked out the door.

"It may be too late," she said to Wolfe and Casey. "Duren has spies. He probably already knows about the strike."

The green eyes said the rest.

~ ~ ~

A quarter-hour later, Wolfe took Casey to the room they were sharing and handcuffed him to the bed. "Beecher's orders," he said with a shrug. Then he returned to the bar to watch what was left of the fight, trade tales with Rusty, and drink a few more gimlets. Ala went to collect her things.

In the dark in his room Casey lay with his eyes open but his mind and body feeling the accumulated exhaustion of the past two weeks. He didn't even have the energy to resent the handcuffs. Beecher was wrong, though. He wasn't going anywhere. He had nowhere to go. He closed his eyes, hoping he could go to sleep and not think. He was tired of thinking. He wanted to drift off into a space as dark as his room.

But this night was no different from the others. He fell into a light sleep, and his mind quickly crowded with the old ghosts, his own ghosts—that night in Jonesboro, the idea that Clyde Point was there and that he pulled the trigger that killed Bux. Orella telling him he had it all

223

wrong, and now he knew it was the truth. He did have it all wrong.

A light knock at the door brought him back to his room in the Red Chief Inn. Then came a second.

"Yeah," Casey called out. "What is it?"

The door opened, and there she stood, the moon to her back.

"Where's Marty?" she asked.

"In the bar," he said to the silhouette facing him.

She stepped into the room, leaving the door open. He watched her become part of the darkness at the foot of the bed. She brought with her a hint of talcum.

"My ride is here. I wanted to tell Marty goodbye."

A moment passed, and she spoke again.

"You came back for me. That night at the bridge."

*She was the one in the rearview mirror. Of course she was.*

"You ask a lot of questions."

"It's not a question."

He listened to her breathe, felt her presence close to him, the scent of talcum so faint he couldn't be sure whether he smelled it or just remembered it.

"You aren't what they thought you were," she said to him. "Orella knew that. You should know it, too."

The darkness emptied, and her silhouette slipped back through the doorway. Then it was gone, and he was alone in his room.

~ ~ ~

Beecher got a summons to the telephone before daybreak the next morning. After he hung up, he stepped back into the dining room, where Wolfe and Casey had joined Berliner at their table at the far end. None of them had wanted breakfast, only coffee plus cigarettes for Wolfe. Berliner declined the writer's offer to buy him a cigar. The old gangster was dressed immaculately for his luncheon with the Big Mahah—white suit, pink shirt, white tie, three point pocket square.

Ala had successfully stopped the strike until Monday morning, Beecher told them. The news calmed Berliner a little, but he was still shaky when he climbed into the Oldsmobile to make the three-hour trip to Moon Lake.

"Don't get any wild ideas," the agent told him. "We're right behind you."

When Beecher got behind the wheel of the Caprice, Wolfe pointed to the bright red tie the agent was wearing.

"What's the Man gonna say?" he asked. With a wink and a grin, the writer turned to Casey in the back. "Hoover doesn't like his agents wearing red ties. Don't ask me why. Beecher's a rogue. What'd I tell you?"

The sun was shining, not a cloud in the sky, and hardly any other cars in sight when Beecher's Caprice pulled onto the road behind the Olds. They were on the outskirts of Jackson when the agent told them the truth about Ala's phone call.

"She can't stop the strike," he said, clearing a frog out of his throat. "Still set for seven this morning. They're all too fired up, she said. She got there too late."

Wolfe studied Beecher's profile for a long time.

"So what does that mean?"

"It means we're going ahead as planned. It's our only shot, and we're taking it."

"So Berliner's walking into a trap."

Beecher stared at the driver of the slow-moving Oldsmobile in front of him, honked the horn for him to speed up.

"To hell with Berliner. We can't turn back now. What happens happens. We're going through with this. Either way, we win. Everything will be on tape, and we can use it." He turned to Wolfe and then nodded toward the Olds. "To hell with him."

Casey listened, remembering Wolfe's description of Beecher. *You can trust him. Right out of the FBI manual— Fidelity, Bravery, and Integrity.* He didn't say anything. None of them did. They rode the long straight highway toward the Delta flatlands in silence.

At one point, Beecher had to punch the horn again to get Berliner to speed up. They could see the fat man stare back at them in the rearview mirror. He looked for a long time, and then he turned his eyes to the road.

# CHAPTER 11

They didn't travel far before Beecher told Wolfe to reach into his glove compartment and pull out the Royal 500 transistor he kept there.

"I want to hear if there's news on this damn strike," he said, the scratch in his voice rougher now, like a straight razor coming down a strop.

"Find Greenwood. This is one reason I'm not in that car with Berliner this part of the trip. I don't like him alone with his thoughts, but he knows what he's got to do, and we've got to know what's going on."

"Tell me again why you can't get AM on the car radio?" Casey asked from the back.

"That's good time radio," Wolfe answered. "J. Edgar doesn't want his men listening to rock 'n' roll when they're supposed to be chasing commies."

"I don't want Berliner listening to it either," Beecher said. "That's why no radio in the Olds."

Casey looked to the road ahead, to the white-suited fat man hunched over his steering wheel. Wolfe looked at Beecher.

"Gettin' a cold?" he asked.

"The sonuvabitch was up all night, couldn't sleep, so I didn't either."

"Hey, who slept?" Wolfe asked. "Five gimlets, and I still stared at the ceiling till daybreak." With a nod to Casey: "So did my roommate, I'm betting."

The writer turned on the radio and tried to find the Greenwood station. What he got was a lot of static, country music, and gospel before he finally found it. Still south of the Yazoo City bluffs where the Delta cotton land begins, the three men bent toward the drawling voice as it read the latest reports on crop projections, the farm bill in Washington, Front Street in Memphis, the commodities exchange in Chicago, the weather. They were thoroughly caught up on farm news by the time the voice filed this breaking story:

> *Just nine days after violence broke out at a union rally resulting in the shooting death of a local policeman, workers at the Bengal Britches garment plant in Spider Creek have gone on strike to protest conditions at the 10-year-old facility, which employs approximately 400. A plant official who asked to remain anonymous said the strike is totally without justification and that it, like the riot*

228

*that preceded it, was provoked by outside agitators. He said the plant has been effectively shut down for the rest of the day. Early this morning picketers lined the gates outside the plant entrance and also along Highway 61, singing songs and carrying signs like "NO UNION, NO WORK," "ON STRIKE FOR WHAT'S RIGHT," "WE'RE HUMAN BEINGS, NOT DOLLAR SIGNS."*

*Percy County Sheriff J. D. Marchand said his deputies and the town's police force are armed and ready if things get out of hand. Here's more of what the sheriff told us about the strike: "I guess they'd rather do this than work. One good man, a true American patriot, has already died because of this communist infiltration into our community."*

*Marchand went on to say 37-year-old Wa-lo-dek Reymont with the New York City-based International Textile Union has been arrested and charged for disrupting the peace. Another strike ringleader, 28-year-old Ala Gadomska, is being sought in connection with both the riot and the death of Spider Creek police officer Grady Turnipseed. The 40-year-old Spider Creek native was shot and killed by an unknown assailant during the July 21st union rally near the plant that featured Gadomska as main speaker. Reymont was also injured during that event. The assailant, who left the scene with Gadomska, is still at large.*

As the news report gave way to a recorded "exclusive" with Congressman Whitten talking about his work on the Agriculture Subcommittee, Wolfe turned the radio off with an angry snap. "What the hell! They're going to try to pin Turnipseed on Ala, too. As for Reymont, he'll never make it out of that jail alive."

Beecher, his face an iron mask, cleared his throat to speak.

"They may be stupid, but Duren's not," he said. "Neither is your niece. She's a step ahead of them. She told me to keep the radio tuned to Greenwood. She made an anonymous call to the station to make sure they had the story. The Spider Creek cops picked up Reymont before she even got there. Getting it on air buys him some life insurance. Look, this whole barrel of rotten fish is about to come crashing down. We're bringing it down. We're seeing this through. All the way."

Wolfe reached for a Lucky, lit it, and fell back in his seat. The mid-morning sun was growing into a giant interrogation lamp, brilliant against a bleached, cloudless sky. In either direction along the highway was a ghostly emptiness, as if they'd entered forbidden territory, closed to all except the Olds and the '58 Caprice following it.

They had taken 49 out of Jackson and were following it through Yazoo City and Greenwood to Clarksdale, bypassing Spider Creek to the east. From Clarksdale they would go west to Highway 1, snaking along the Mississippi River to Moon Lake. Just before reaching Moon Lake they would stop at an abandoned church at the edge of the little town of Friar's Point. Here they would go over the plan one last time.

The sun shimmered across Casey's closed eyelids as he laid his head against the seat, imagined the bald-headed tamale maker and his niece marching and singing outside the plant gates. He couldn't imagine what they would be singing.

The Olds plodded along Highway 49 as if it were going up a steep hill. Beecher would punch the horn now and then, and the fat man would speed up for a few miles but then slip back to the 45-to-50 range. Shoulders pulled in, arms drawn close to his sides, head tilted downward, little eyes peering up at the rear view mirror when Beecher got close on his tail or blew the horn, he drove like the condemned man that he was.

Before long they were in the middle of a sea of cotton, with little islands here and there—gins, graineries, shotgun shacks, brick bungalows, old growth cypress, oak, and gum along meandering creeks and bayous where the water never moved. It was an endless drive to Clarksdale, but once they got on the narrow strip of road that was Highway 1, the mood in the Caprice changed. Wolfe chain-smoked. Beecher worked his jaw muscles. Casey listened to the acid rumbling in his belly.

It was noon when they reached Friar's Point. Berliner pulled to the side to let the Caprice lead the way. They drove past two-story, white-framed houses and a couple Civil War historical markers into an area of cinder block porches and makeshift garages. At the end of the line was the white-plastered church with the red steeple that was their stopping point. The church windows were broken out. Graffiti mocked Jesus, God, and the police. Just behind the church was a picnic table in a small grove of cottonwood. The cars pulled onto the grounds, up to the grove, and emptied.

The men gathered around the table.

"I gotta piss," mumbled Berliner, pale as a dead man.

Beecher nodded toward the trees, and the old gangster shuffled off into them. They waited and then watched him as he returned, his gait slow and labored. The agent propped his leg on the table's seating board and crossed his arms over his knee.

"To accomplish our mission we need more than the testimonies of a whorehouse operator and a cop-killer. We need to hear Duren's guilt pour from his own mouth, let him tie enough rope around his neck to hang himself." He stopped and glared at the man whose job it was to make such testimony possible. "Berliner, stop staring at the ground and look me in the eye. Your life is on the line. If you fail, this operation not only collapses, you'll be trapped. Duren will feed you to his auger, and we don't want that, do we? Every sweet lie you ever told a whore is nothing compared to the sweetness that's got to come out of your mouth today. I've got a lot of confidence in you. You were born for this performance. You've had a lifetime of rehearsals."

Berliner raised his eyes and searched the faces of the men around the table. "She didn't stop the strike, did she?"

Beecher ignored the question and pulled out of his pocket a small box-like instrument, about three inches by two inches, roughly the size of a cigarette case.

"This is the transmitter that I'm going to attach to your groin area. It'll be taped to your shorts and will transmit everything that's said in the restaurant to a radio head in the car. It's a perfect setup because out here there's nothing to interfere with transmission. No concrete, no steel, nothing."

The agent walked to a loose-hinged door at the rear of the church. Opening it with no trouble, he motioned to Berliner to follow him in. Casey and Wolfe exchanged looks. A few minutes later, the two emerged again, Berliner adjusting his pants, Beecher resuming his spot at the head of the table. He told Berliner to go and wait in the Olds and turned to Wolfe. "What you say, writer? All those years we thought we'd lost this fella, and now here we are. You're about to get the scoop of a lifetime, put this Federation and its Nazi Mahah on the front page."

He paused, long enough for Wolfe to ask, "What you thinkin'?"

"I'm thinking of the men and women in uniform who died because of Duren, the blueprints and shipping schedules that he and others stole during the war. I'm remembering that Duren's not the only Werewolf still out there."

"Thought you were retiring after this job."

The agent shrugged, looked at his watch.

"We're getting close to one o'clock. We don't want to be late for Max's party. Just remember everything we've said. A couple miles up Lula Road is an old shack that used to be a bait shop. That's where we'll set up. It's far enough away to keep from being spotted and close enough for the radio to pick up what's going on. Berliner will continue on to the Nest, less than an eighth of a mile. He knows what to do. Once he's done, we meet back here at this church."

He checked his watch again. "It's time."

They rose from their seats and went back to the cars. Beecher said a last few words to Berliner before climbing back into the Caprice. He made some adjustments on the radio head, and off they went, back to Highway 1, where they turned north.

After a mile or two they reached Lula Road, which followed the Moon Lake crescent all the way to the Nest. Letting Berliner get far enough ahead to prevent anyone making a connection between the two cars, Beecher drove slowly, passing cabins on the left nestled among the cypress trees that bordered the lake. To the right were mostly cotton fields and untended land with little more than brush and weed growing in the sandy loam and buckshot. They passed a small grocery store that advertised a meal of fresh catfish, rooster fries, and hush puppies for a buck fifty.

Farther up the road, in the middle of a field, was the boarded-up, tree-shrouded bait shop that Beecher had described. Clearly visible in the flat, open landscape ahead was the rambling two-story, wood-framed restaurant. Beecher eased onto a dirt path leading to the shack and came to a stop within its shadows.

Pulling out his binoculars, he stepped out of the Caprice and moved to a spot where he could watch the Olds as it made its way up the road and finally onto the gravel lot in front of the Nest. Already on the lot was a large black New Yorker, sleek and shiny as a panther, parked between a red Cadillac and a Chevy Bel Air with a red light on top.

"You see what I see?" Beecher asked after Wolfe had taken the binoculars.

The writer nodded.

"Duren has invited some friends. I figure they got the place to themselves today."

A lean man in a dark suit waited on the Nest's pea-green, wraparound porch. Across the road was a long, sagging wooden pier with a large sign nailed to a post at the entrance. "Danger—No Trespass, " the sign warned. At its far end, where the pilings had collapsed, the pier disappeared into the lake.

Beecher motioned for them to return to the Caprice. Once inside, he reached across the seat and opened the dashboard. Inside were two guns. He picked up the larger of the two.

"This is a Turkish-made Krikkale, a World War II-era collector's item, in perfect shape, a double-action, self-loading variation of the German Walther." He handed it to

Wolfe. "You may need this." With his right hand resting just above the open dashboard, he turned to Casey.

"You probably know this without me telling you, but this is a snub-nosed Colt, what we call a detective special. Like the other, it's loaded and ready for use." He closed the dashboard—the gun still in it--without saying any more.

Sounds were coming out of the radio—Berliner climbing out of the Olds, his heavy breathing.

"He's waiting," said the man on the porch, his German accent clear and distinct in the radio.

Casey thought he recognized the voice.

"That's Klaus. I met that guy at the Peabody." *He's waiting. It's what Klaus said that day, too.*

"Yeah, Duren's manservant," Wolfe said, nodding. "Been with him since the old days. They have a special relationship, those two, the part of all this that Kettle and the others find most distasteful, I imagine."

"What are you talking about?" Casey asked.

"Inversion. An old tradition in the German officer corps. Duren never wore a uniform, but with his man Friday and his Schmiss, he can imagine himself an officer of the highest standing, *Gauleiter* of the United States South."

"His what?"

"Schmiss, the scar on his cheek. German fraternity boys prove their manhood by dueling with sabers. Getting cut is a badge of honor. Duren got his in Munich."

236

Beecher motioned for silence as the front door to the Nest opened and voices came across the radio. One voice, angry and shrill, overpowered the others.

"Diese verdammte Jüdin, kommunistische Dreck! Wieder auf ihrer Bühne!"

"What the hell is he saying?" Casey asked as he leaned between Beecher and Wolfe in the front.

"He's talking about Gadomska, lamenting the fact that the damned Jew and communist filth is back on her stage again!" Beecher answered as another voice came out of the radio in response to Duren's tirade.

"We'll find her, Mr. Duren. Don't you worry. We'll take care of it."

"Marchand," Wolfe whispered.

"Yes, you'll take care of it, you idiot! Like that officer did at the rally that was supposed to make an end of all this. Now we have this so-called strike. Strike! I fought these Red Fronters, these Bolsheviks, in Munich in 1919. You think I will put up with this in my own factory?"

Beecher turned to Wolfe. "He thinks she's behind the strike."

The three in the Caprice listened as Duren's rage poured through the radio, loud and bitter and sarcastic, all at the same time. The Nazi was apparently moving about the room, given the shifting volume of his voice and the repeated knocks of his cane on the floor. Duren had yet to acknowledge Berliner's presence, but the men in the Caprice could hear the fat man's nervous breathing. When

237

Duren said the word "strike," the breathing actually stopped for several seconds.

"And let me tell you this," the Big Mahah bellowed, "my partner in New Orleans is going to be very upset. Do you have any idea what happens to our plans if he pulls out?"

Beecher and Wolfe looked at each other with the same question on their faces.

"He doesn't need to find out, Mr. Duren," Marchand tried to assure him.

"What do you mean? I've heard the radio reports."

"That was the Polack's work, Mr. Duren," said another in the room, the voice of a relatively young man, educated and polished. "She called the radio station before I could put a lid on it, but we're killing this story, I assure you."

"You idiot son of an idiot!" Duren shouted at the man. "You don't even understand your own business! Once it's out, it's out! You can't kill it!"

The younger man wasn't shaken by the attack. "That may be true anywhere else, Mr. Duren, but not here, not in our world. The story is dead, I promise you."

Tate Kettle's familiar drawl made itself heard for the first time. "Junior's right, Max. Let me remind you, we know how to take care of things like that down here. And take this to the bank, once the story's dead, the strike is dead. Got nowhere to go."

Kettle's assurance managed to douse Duren's fiery tirade, allowing time for the German to turn to his new visitor. The men in the car listened as the knock against the hardwood floor grew louder. Duren was approaching.

"Ah, our friend from Alabama, Mr. Berliner, all dressed in white." The third syllable of "Alabama" popped like the sound of a small-caliber pistol. Berliner was "Bare-lean-err," and once again his breathing stopped. Duren was close. He seemed to be speaking into the hidden mike.

"Albrecht prefers to be called Ike. Such an ugly name. Albrecht believes he will make us a lot of money, don't you, Albrecht? Certainly you know Mr. Kettle, but do you know my other friends, Sheriff Marchand, Mr. Washburn the publisher? I summoned them here as soon as I heard what was happening at my factory. Gentlemen, Albrecht here is a very established man. From Litzmannstadt, what the Poles call `Woodge' in their impossible language. He advises me in my textile investments. He knows textiles, casinos, politics, whores. Mostly he knows whores. However, Albrecht, I'm afraid, is a very poor judge of people, isn't that right, Albrecht? Why do I say that? It's because of him I hired the half-ape, half-nigger who was unable to kill the Jüdin."

A quarter mile away, Beecher slapped his hands and rubbed them in delight. "Perfect! Exactly what we need!"

Casey was pokerfaced.

"Yes, I have Mr. Berliner here to thank for this Schweinerei. Don't I, Albrecht?" Duren continued. "Don't I have you and your late friend Clyde Point to thank?"

239

The Big Mahah drew even closer to Berliner. Their breathing was like a radio duet, one steady and resolute, the other broken by tiny peeps, the fits and starts of unraveled nerves. The radio filled with static as Berliner stepped back and pulled or adjusted his pants.

"I'll crucify the bastard if he pulls that transmitter loose," Beecher growled under his breath.

"Gentlemen, I have another reason to thank Albrecht. This ape I mentioned is actually still alive, and, imagine, in the company of an FBI agent and some journalist. I know this because I have friends I trust who tell me these things. Albrecht, however, told me the ape was dead. Albrecht lied. Why would you lie to me, Albrecht?"

Beecher turned to Wolfe, his eyes filled with something the writer wasn't sure he'd ever seen in them before: dismay.

"Nix talked. So he is part of it. How long? I never figured … "

Wolfe could only shake his head.

Casey stared at the radio, spellbound by Duren's voice.

"Albrecht." Mock concern dripped from each syllable. "You look horrible. What is wrong? What is the matter with you? You're sweating like a pig, and you're so pale. Are you sick?"

"Max, you shouldn't blame me … " The Berliner soprano was that of a wounded animal, desperate yet helpless before its prey.

240

"Gentlemen, I think Albrecht is worried. I must admit I'm quite disappointed in him, even angry. Yes, I am very angry." He stopped to laugh, a grim, humorless laugh. "Not that I worry about some FBI loner operating without the approval of his superiors."

"How does he …?" Beecher blurted.

"Or about his writer friend, a nothing who works for a third-rate nothing magazine? What can they do to me? No, no, Albrecht. It's not these untermenschen who concern me. It's you."

Duren was standing close enough to Berliner that the radio picked up the brush of their coats against one another. "You're very fat, Albrecht, aren't you? Even fatter than the last time I saw you. You're soft and decadent. Your lust for women and food and wine has been your undoing, I'm afraid."

"Max, I … I …"

In the Caprice, Wolfe wiped sweat from his face. "I don't like this. This is a tribunal. Maybe we should … ."

"No!" Beecher snapped with a quick shake of his head.

He hardly had time to turn back to the radio before they heard a voice from outside. "Get out of the car!"

The three turned to see two men in dark suits—like Klaus's—with guns pointed. They were standing to the left and right of the Caprice's rear fender. Far behind them, parked to the side of Lula Road, was a black Dodge.

"Out, goddamit, and I mean now!" barked the one to the left.

241

Beecher's eyes locked on Wolfe's as his hand slipped to the .38 holstered on his waist. He had it out before his other hand reached the door handle. Wolfe gripped the Krikkale in his lap and swung around, and it was as if that moment they became a human double-action/single-action weapon. The car doors opened, and the .38 and Krikkale fired simultaneously. The suits were down, down before they could even get a good look at the men they'd ordered out of the car.

"What was that?" a voice in the Nest shouted. It was Washburn.

"It's all right," Duren cooed. "Just my men taking care of a situation I anticipated. Albrecht, you look as if you are about to faint."

An ugly pause followed in which neither man breathed. Then Duren, icily: "Klaus, search this man."

A determined rustling of clothes followed, interspersed with Berliner's distraught grunts and groans. Hands ran briskly along bunched fabric, snapping a belt, popping a button, until another outburst came from Duren.

"Verräter!"

Wolfe, having made sure the gunmen were dead, caught Duren's voice just as he climbed back in the Caprice.

"'Traitor'," he translated. "The unforgivable sin. We go in now, or Berliner's a dead man."

As the writer checked his gun, Beecher grabbed his coat lapel and shook it back and forth. "No!" the agent barked, and the moment he did the radio went dead. The three stared at the machine, transfixed by its silence until the sound of a loud shot arced across the cotton fields. It came from the Nest and was quickly followed by another.

Beecher fired the Caprice, rammed it into gear, and spun out of the dirt path with squealing wheels, past the dead suits, the parked Dodge, and onto Lula Road. He raced the eighth-mile to where the restaurant's peaceful exterior gave no hint of the violence inside.

Within seconds the Caprice had swung onto the lot and come to a dust-shrouded stop just behind the New Yorker, blocking it from an easy exit and spitting clouds of Delta dirt onto its immaculate blackness. Beecher immediately pushed open the door and turned to Wolfe and Casey.

"Marty, you come with me. Eubanks, you sit tight, keep your eyes on the exits."

The agent pulled the still-warm Hoover Heater out of his holster and ran in a half-crouch toward the house, Wolfe following closely behind. Casey climbed to the front seat, grabbed the detective special out of the dashboard, and watched as they bounded up the steps and onto the porch. Beecher glanced toward a second exit at the north end and signaled Casey by pointing at it. The shades of the restaurant's windows were all pulled. After Beecher picked the front door lock, the two men disappeared inside.

The moment they were gone Casey felt a surging impulse to ignore Beecher's order and rush in behind them. He opened the car door and swung partially out. As his eyes moved along the row of windows on the porch, he heard an explosion of shots from inside the Nest.

On its heels came the sounds of furious motion, falling furniture, shouts and cries. Casey jumped out of the Caprice and leaped around the door to just left of the front fender, an impotent rage grating at the point in the pit in his belly where he'd always figured his ulcer was. He felt the impotence even as he held Beecher's loaded Colt in his right hand. He understood the order. Yes, Beecher wanted the exits watched, but more importantly he wanted the car and the incriminating testimony on the radio tape protected.

A second volley of shots came from inside.

Beecher and Wolfe were in a standoff. A glance at the door at the porch's north end paid in spades when out rushed Max "The Big Mahah" Duren, cane-less, pistol in hand, the white shirt under his black suspenders soaked in sweat and sprayed with blood.

Now he was the hunted animal, and it was all over his face and in his eyes as he scanned the cars, trying to penetrate the blinding rays from the sun overhead. He rushed down the steps, dragging his bad leg with him like Chester Goode in *Gunsmoke*.

The German hurried toward the New Yorker, stumbling and falling once but then climbing up off the ground with grunting determination. He was more nimble than Casey imagined. Duren hadn't yet spotted Casey, who had moved beyond the Caprice front fender to the rear of the Bel Air. The moment the old Nazi reached his sleek black panther he slumped against the hood for support, and when he did, he saw the source of his tribulations. Their eyes met for the first time since their encounter at the Peabody.

For a hollow, timeless second, Casey didn't recognize the crazed creature in front of him, so different from the man in the oriental robe with his yellow cigarette and walking stick. That was the second Duren raised his pistol, shook it at Casey with the cry "You! You!" on his lips, and fired, once, twice, three times, missing wildly.

Casey ducked behind the Bel Air and heard the German fumbling furiously with the door of his New Yorker. Casey thought of something Duren likely had forgotten until that very moment: Klaus, the driver, had the keys, and Klaus was inside the restaurant, maybe dead by now. Just then they both heard another car rush onto the increasingly crowded gravel lot. Casey looked behind him and saw a familiar red-and-white '55 Ford Crown Victoria with a tall strawberry blonde in the driver's seat.

"No!" he growled loud enough for the German to hear.

"Die Jüdin!" Duren shouted.

Casey peeped over the trunk of the Bel Air and saw the Big Mahah take aim at Ala.

"Hell, no, you don't!" he shouted, jumping up, his Colt pointed at the Nazi. Duren swung around and fired, this time hitting his mark directly in the chest. He tried to shoot again but the chamber was empty.

Casey fell to his knee, cursing himself for being so dumb as to catch a bullet from as bad a shot as Max Duren. His chest went numb the moment of impact, but he sensed a rising and ominous tide deep within himself. In a protest against the illogic of his wound, he pulled himself to his feet, lifted the snub-nosed Colt, but the scar-faced Nazi was, by this time, racing, against all logic, toward the ancient pier across Lula Road. Forcing himself after his prey, Casey made his way to and across Lula Road, past the "Danger—No Trespass" sign to the edge of the pier. He could hear Ala Gadomska running behind him shouting, "Casey! Casey!"

Duren stood at the far end of the pier, close to the point where the pilings had sunk into the black waters of Moon Lake. The Nazi's panic had driven him to a point of no return, as if he expected a U-boat to arrive and whisk him away. He stood near the water's edge with his empty, useless pistol, facing the *half-ape, half-nigger* who had brought him to this.

A split moment into the face-off, Duren's eyes shifted toward The Nest and bulged with terror. In the distance beyond, Casey heard a cacophony of running feet. As heavy as it was at that point, he lifted the Colt again and aimed it at Duren's head. The German backed away, step upon step, toward Moon Lake until he fell with a loud shriek into the ink-like water. Slapping his arms up and down, he cried out, "Hilfe! Hilfe! Kann nicht schwimmen!" and then he sank, so quickly that it was as if the lake had sucked him into its depths.

Casey dropped the gun without ever firing it and fell onto the pier's rotting floor, his head just missing a raised nail. The sun overhead faded as a fog from somewhere within drifted upwards across his consciousness. He could hear a faraway voice, a woman's voice.

"Casey!" she cried. "Casey!"

He could barely hear it, but as soon as he did, light appeared within the fog. He imagined a gray procession— Bux Baggett, faceless dead men, and, at the end of it, Orella. This time he knew it was Orella, and it was her voice calling him. He wanted to answer but he couldn't make a sound. The fog was too thick, and soon it turned into a deep and endless night.

# CHAPTER 12

Martin Wolfe stood at the grave for more than an hour after the preacher finished. The sky was overcast, and clouds thickened in the distance. The grave was in a lonely corner of the White Hill Presbyterian Church Cemetery, where a stand of pines gave way to unending acres of tobacco that had already gone through the first couple of primings. The gravediggers had lowered the wooden casket into the earth, covered it with dirt, and left with the preacher. One of them mumbled they'd be back later to finish the job. They'd watched the rumbling clouds the entire time, the distant lightning.

On either side of the grave stood a metal stand holding a wreath of mixed flowers. Wolfe bought one, Ala the other. She couldn't come to the service because the International Textile Union had called organizers to its New York headquarters to discuss the proposed abandonment of the Southern campaign. Memories of Operation Dixie were still fresh and painful, and the failed election at Spider Creek was just another nail in the latest campaign's own coffin. Ala wanted to keep fighting.

A small metal nameplate at the foot of Casey's grave told who was buried there. Wolfe had made a round of calls. Gin Smith said he'd talk to the boys down at Pokey's pool hall about a collection for a headstone. Myrt and Blue Critchfield wouldn't answer the phone or the door. None of them came to the service.

It lasted barely twenty minutes. A Pentecostal preacher from Orella's church presided.

"'Foxes have holes and birds of the air have nests, but the Son of man hath not where to lay his head,'" he told the gathering of one plus the gravediggers. Luke 9. "Casey Eubanks, a wandering man all his life, finally has a place to lay his head."

When Wolfe did the sign of the cross, the preacher's lips curled just slightly. Wolfe had tried to tell him a little of the deceased's story, but the preacher said he knew plenty enough about Casey Eubanks.

The writer slipped his fingers under his shirt and touched the wooden Joseph as he stared down at the stirred earth, the sandy soil so good for the cash crop that stretched to the horizon beyond the cemetery.

"I got you as close to your woman as I could," he said, and he had the crazy sensation Casey was listening. Wolfe believed in those things. She was just a few rows away. So was Bux. They all shared the same earth now.

The long journey back to White Hill had given him time to think. Beecher was recuperating from the wound to the shoulder that he'd gotten from Klaus before taking the German down with his Hoover Heater.

Wolfe would never forget the scene inside the Nest— Marchand and Washburn cowering behind an overturned table; Kettle, neutralized with his nose at the serious end of a Krikkale barrel; Berliner's agonized face as the life ebbed out of him. Before making his escape through the rear door, Duren had fired twice point blank into the fat man's belly, adding to the two bullets Klaus had already put there.

After the Big Mahah fell into Moon Lake crying he couldn't swim, Wolfe had gone in after him, but the man was nowhere to be found. The local authorities dragged that end of the lake, belatedly and half-heartedly, and they searched its surroundings but turned up nothing. The agent's files showed Alois Dürren was an excellent swimmer, despite his bad leg. He'd even won awards at Ludwig-Maximilians University in Munich. The old Nazi was probably en route to his partner in New Orleans.

In his hospital room, Beecher also had time to think, and he was fine-tuning a theory that the partner was none other than Ernst Kapuze, Duren's Kamerad in South America and later New York, another Werewolf on the loose, one even craftier than Duren and, more than likely, Duren's superior in the Federation. This was an idea Beecher had bandied about with Wolfe in times past but which had died for lack of evidence. Duren's comment in The Nest resurrected it.

However, the agent would have to free-lance if he were going to go after Ernst Kapuze. His days with the Bureau were over. His blue-flamer SAC had sent him notification in the hospital. Beecher had suspected a letter of censure wouldn't be enough to mollify J. Edgar in a situation like this. Even a transfer to Butte wasn't sufficient for a rogue like Hardy Beecher. The agent told the SAC's emissary that he already had his fishing gear ready and to spare the gold watch.

Somehow none of it mattered. A final ember died inside Beecher when he heard Duren talk about the FBI loner who didn't have his agency's blessing. With that ember went any real hope that the questioning facing Kettle, Washburn, and Marchand was going to produce anything. The best lawyers in Memphis had already lined up for the defense. Marchand even claimed he was simply at The Nest doing his own investigation.

The events at Moon Lake did make the front pages in the Memphis, Jackson, and even Spider Creek newspapers, below the fold, but then the story disappeared. It was full of holes anyway, with little incentive to fill them, all about a crooked business deal gone bad between a shadowy, German-born, Memphis-based financier and an Alabama roadhouse owner, and the shooting death of an alleged cop-killer being used by the FBI as an informant in its investigation of the financier.

Duren's friends at the scene got barely a mention, and his taped revelations got none. Beecher's no comment was Bureau policy, of course. Wolfe was doing his own story. Why help the competition? *Labor* would publish it in its September edition, a first-person account with a detailed description of what was known about the Federation and its connection to Nazi fugitives. Beecher cashed in an IOU at the Bureau to get a 20-year-old FBI drawing of Duren for the piece.

After securing his scoop, Wolfe planned to contact a reporter for the *New York Times* named Sitton and see if he might be interested in pursuing the story while giving a little credit to *Labor* along the way.

Certainly the Bureau had no interest in pursuing the case. Senate Judiciary Committee Chairman James O. "Big Jim" Eastland did, however, and he wasted no time calling for yet another congressional hearing on communist influence behind labor activities in the Deep South. The Memphis newspaper said Tate Kettle was scheduled as a witness. What was going to happen to the workers at Bengal Britches was anyone's guess.

Wolfe felt the first big drops of the storm to come. The clouds were rolling in now across the sky's ashen gloominess. A hard wind blew through the pines. A littering of faded plastic flowers, paper wrapping, wreaths, and twisted wiring bunched up against the trees. Some of the wrapping blew out across the tobacco fields.

The writer looked down at Casey and wanted to offer a final benediction, but nothing came to him. So he turned and walked away. Passing Orella's grave, he stopped and reached for a Lucky. It was his last. Lighting up, he looked at the pack before crushing it in his hand. LSMFT, the slogan went. "'Lucky Strikes Mean Fine Tobacco.' Damned cancer sticks going to kill me someday."

He blew an imperfect smoke ring into the wind's direction and recalled those last moments he saw Casey alive. He was on that rotten pier, pointing Beecher's little detective special directly at Max Duren's head. He had him in his sights, finally, after everything that had happened, but he never fired, just like he never fired that shot at Ala. In the end he'd even taken the shot meant for her.

Wolfe looked down at Orella's grave. She, too, only had a metal nameplate. Not enough time for a headstone.

"Had him in his sights and never fired. Took the shot meant for Ala. What do you know? But that wouldn't have surprised you. Am I right?"

*The End*

## Author's Acknowledgements

This novel was long in the making, and many people helped in the process. First of all, my wife Suzanne Centenio Atkins was a supportive presence throughout, as were our children Rachel Atkins, Michael Atkins, Andy Gates, and Jessica Byrd. My writer friends Jere Hoar and Ace Atkins kept me going when my faith sometimes flagged. Wordsmith Jere helped keep the writing honest and spare. Ace made suggestions that were key to plot development and pacing. Certainly my publisher James L. Dickerson and cover artist Eric Summers deserve special mention. Others whose help was invaluable include in no certain order and at the risk of leaving many names out: Neil White, John Hailman, John Lavoie, Danny Forsyth, Robin Street, Wlodek and Ala Kopycki, Jordan Zjawiony, Bob Mayton, Fred Watson, Jim Ewing, Lewis Atkins, John Atkins, Evi Womble, the late Marilyn Tapscott Atkins, my late parents Roger and Maria Atkins, and my late grandparents Minnie and Fletcher Atkins. The rich garden of Atkins family tales and legends provided the seed that became *Casey's Last Chance*.